Night of the Cossack

Dan,
Blessings to you.
Tom Blubaugh
Prov. 12:9, 19:21

an imprint of Bound by Faith Publishers

Night of the Cossack

original cover art by Jeremy Sams

Night of the Cossack

Published by Bound by Faith Publishers

International Standard Book Number 978-0-9829029-2-9

Printed in the United States of America 2011

www.boundbyfaithpublishers.com

Toll Free 877-731-4550

To my beautiful wife and helpmate,

Barbara Holmes, without your support,

I could not have written this novel.

Acknowledgements

I gratefully acknowledge Michelle Buckman, who started me down the path of writing serious fiction and removed the fear of being critiqued. I have benefited from the Springfield Writers Workshop, in particular Katherine Chaudhri, Beverly Crandell, Nancy Dailey, Kay Galliger, Louise Jackson, Charles King, Dr. Deborah Kukal, Debbie Morris, Suzanne Walker-Pocheco, Beverly Reid, and Toni Somers for devoting substantial time to critiquing my writing. Special thanks goes to Melissa Tweedel for editing and correcting my grammar.

Introduction

My grandfather died of Lou Gehrigs disease in 1941, in the same hospital where I was born in 1942. I've always regretted being deprived of knowing him. When I was a child, I spent a week each summer at my grandmother's house. Above the television, hanging on the gold wallpaper, were two oval, mahogany frames protecting two beautiful pictures. The picture on the right displayed a lovely young woman with long, wavy, jet-black hair—my grandmother. The picture on the left was my grandfather, a man with a soft, pleasant round face, a receding hairline, and a partial smile.

My grandmother never talked about my grandfather that I recall. As I grew older, I learned a few things about him, but nothing that really told me who he was. I never understood this. Perhaps it was because I never asked questions in spite of my interest. I've always been aware of the emptiness of not having a grandfather. My grandmother passed away when I was sixteen. Little did I know that any hope of discovering substantive information about my grandfather died with her.

As I grew older, I'd ask my mother and her siblings about him, but no one seemed to know much about his past, and what they did remember conflicted with each other's memories. Together my grandparents spoke nine languages. They wanted their children to be Americans; so when they spoke of the old countries, they spoke in a language their children didn't understand. She was from Poland, and he was from Russia.

None of their sons had children, therefore, my grandfather's name did not continue. He seemed like a ghost.

All of their children, three sons and three daughters, have passed away except my Aunt Sarah. After my mother passed away, I sat down with my aunt and asked her every question I could think of, gleaning every detail I could. I then began to research the history of the time of my grandparents immigration to the United States. I found pieces of information that made the bits of truth I had already learned make sense. He had been a Russian Cossack soldier in the Ukraine, immigrating to America in 1910.

Writing this story has pushed my imagination to the limit. I wonder what my life might be like had my grandparents not come to America. Would my grandmother have been a victim of Hitler's furnaces like the majority of her family? Would my grandparents still have met and married? Would I be a Polish or Ukrainian citizen—or an immigrant? Let me introduce you to my grandfather as I imagine him.

Chapter 1

Nathan's eyes flew open. Sounds, screams and gunshots penetrated the cold air of his upstairs bedroom. The pungent smell of smoke invaded his nose. He coughed. *Am I having a nightmare?* Shadows danced wildly across the ceiling and down the walls.

Heart pounding, he threw off his covers, jumped out of bed, and rushed to the window. His little brother, Israel, followed.

Its real!

"What is it, Nathan?" Israel whispered.

Nathan pulled his brother against the wall behind him.

"Hey! I want to see!"

"Shush, Israel." Nathan looked through the window at the valley below, his heart racing. Men in long coats and fur hats were running through the village brandishing swords and raising rifles. *Cossacks!*

The Bukolovs' and the Gorbenkos' houses were burning. Bodies lay on the ground. He couldn't tell who they were, but he knew they were friends.

Momma rushed into the room. "Get away from that window, Nathan!"

"Those are Cossack soldiers, Momma!"

"Cossacks," echoed Israel.

"Get dressed, Nathan. Hurry."

Nathan hesitated at the window.

"Now!" she shouted, grabbing him with such force he lost his balance. "Get dressed. Bring your coat."

Nathan turned from the window.

Momma pulled Israel's clothes from the hook behind the door, hurried him into them, and down the stairs.

Nathan shoved his trembling hands into his shirt, the horrible scenes replaying in his mind—houses ablaze, soldiers on horseback, dead bodies, his friends in terror. *Why are the Cossacks here? What do they want?*

He pushed his feet into his boots, jumped up, and hurried to the chest at the foot of the bed. Lifting the lid, he pulled out a knife in its sheath and shoved it into his right boot. He reached back for a leather bag containing lead balls and patches, and a powder horn. He fastened the pouch and powder horn to his belt. The firelight danced across his father's pistol. He picked up the gun and balanced it in his right hand. *Momma said I can't use it until I'm older. She doesn't know I've taken it out when I've gone hunting and practiced shooting it. I'm sixteen. I'm a man. Why should I have to wait?* The thought calmed him.

Nathan shoved the unloaded gun into his belt, went back to the window, and stared at the nightmare below. He turned away and tried to close his mind against the violence. His rifle, loaded and ready to fire leaned against the wall in the corner. He slipped his arm through the sling, hefted the rifle on his shoulder, and grabbed his coat. He ran down the stairs.

The back door banged in the cold January wind. Nathan pushed his right shoulder against the door and forced his way through. A bitter gust whipped down from the Caucasus Mountains and hit him full in the face, pushing him off balance.

Nathan gasped as acrid fumes attacked his nose and stung his eyes. He blinked away the tears and peered through the smoke. Momma moved like a ghost across the yard, her robe billowing behind her. Her long, black hair blew wildly in the wind. She was only halfway across the yard pulling Israel by the hand. *Why isn't she already in the root cellar?* Then he knew the answer—she had waited until he was out of the house.

Nathan lowered his head and fought his way after her. A few meters from the cellar, he froze when he heard the piercing squeal of his terrified horse. He turned toward the barn. "Aza, I'm here. I'm coming," he yelled.

Before he reached the barn a woman's scream ran a chill up his spine. The sound was cut short, followed by an ominous silence. Nathan felt sick. *Momma?*

He glanced toward the cellar. He couldn't see Momma or Israel. Fearing the worst, he turned and stumbled toward the underground room. His eyes still stinging, he stumbled to the entrance, using his rifle as a crutch to keep him upright.

"Momma?" he whispered.

Silence. His heart stopped.

"I hear you, Nathan. We're all right."

Nathan staggered down the steps with relief. His mind swirled with images and terrible sounds. His thoughts returned to Aza. He turned back to the steps.

"Nathan, stay here!"

"I must go to Aza, Momma. I heard him scream. He's panicked, he could hurt himself."

"What can you do for him, Nathan?"

"I can calm him down and turn him loose into the woods. If they set the barn on fire, he'll die. He'll be safe in the woods. I must go!"

"You're more important than your horse. I, we need you here with us. Stay, Nathan. I couldn't bear to lose you."

Nathan was torn. Breathing a heavy sigh in resignation as he pulled the cellar door shut, he let his eyes adjust to the dark. He leaned his rifle against the wall.

Momma wrapped her arms around her older son. Nathan felt her shiver. He knew she was more afraid than cold. *Had she heard the scream?*

She sank to her knees, pulling Nathan down. "I know you're afraid," she whispered.

Nathan tensed. "I'm not afraid. I'm a man—the man of the house. You've said this yourself." He pulled away from her. "You say I'm brave and strong. You tell me I'm like Papa, but you treat me like a little boy."

"Nathan, you're both. You're my little boy, but at the same time you're a man. Can you understand?"

Ignoring her question he said, "Papa should be here to protect us. I didn't even get to tell him good-bye."

"Don't be angry, Nathan. He loved you very much. He loved all of us." She slipped her arms around him again saying, "It was an accident. There was no chance for anyone to say good-bye. Dying wasn't his choice. You're a man, Nathan. You look just like him—tall and strong, yet gentle. You have his black, wavy hair, hazel eyes, even his strong chin. What would I do without you?"

Nathan didn't say anything. He couldn't stay mad at her. Her soft voice melted his heart. *Even when she's afraid, she comforts me. Momma's right. About all of it. It isn't her fault Papa died.*

His anger, no longer directed at her, receded.

"Momma, are we going to be all right?" asked Israel.

"I pray we will, son. Who can know with certainty?"

"I'm scared, Momma," Israel said.

"I know, son, I know."

Nathan felt her arms leave him. In a few seconds, he felt her rocking against him. He knew she was holding Israel.

The woman's scream crept into Nathan's mind again. He put his hands over his ears as if he could silence it. *Was it Vasile's mother?*

Vasile was his best friend. It didn't matter to Vasile that Nathan was a Jew. The two of them hunted elk, roe deer, wild boar, rabbit, and birds almost every day and rode their horses all over the surrounding countryside. They raced. Aza was faster and Nathan always won. *Where is Vasile? Is he alive? Is he hiding in his cellar? Does he have his rifle?*

Nathan was the better shot even though he was two years younger. The men in the village used to wager on which boy would bring in the most game.

The wind howling through the spaces in the cellar door pulled Nathan from his thoughts. He realized he couldn't dwell on Vasile and his family. It was too painful.

His thoughts turned toward the village. Gagra sat at the base of the Caucasus Mountains in northern Georgia, on the eastern shore of the Black Sea. Tonight was one of the rare times the mountains let the Arctic winds assault the village. *The Cossacks seem to have blown in like a whirlwind. Why have they attacked us? What is here that they want? Women? Food? Weapons? Many of the houses are already damaged and there are few families.*

Nathan stroked the handle of Papa's pistol. His father found it after the Turks raided the village. He told Nathan a Turkish soldier must have dropped the gun. The rifle and ammunition bag were gifts to Papa from a woman who lost her husband during the raid. That was when Papa became the village hunter. *I'm the hunter now.*

A strong gust rattled the cellar door, startling Nathan. When it died down, he could hear the terror of the night—constant gunfire, men cursing, women wailing. The sight of the burning houses flooded his mind again. *Please God, don't let them burn our house.*

Time crept past. The gunfire died down and the yells ceased. Suddenly, there was the sound of hoofbeats on the road—many horses at a gallop. The sound faded into the night.

"Momma, I think the Cossacks have gone. I'll see if it's safe now."

"No, son." She pulled Nathan to her and held him tight. "Wait a few minutes more. Maybe the fires will die down."

"The wind's too strong, Momma," he protested. "The fires will burn all night. I need to see." He tried to pull away from her.

She tightened her hold on him. "What can you do if it isn't safe, Nathan?"

What can I do? I must do what Papa would do. I must be a man like Papa. "I'll be careful," he said pulling free of her.

He reached for his rifle, crept up the steps, and pushed the door open just enough to see into the yard. The fires from the burning village houses cast an eerie glow on the thick smoke swirling in the wind. He breathed a sigh of relief as he realized their home was still standing.

"The house and barn look to be all right," he whispered to his mother. "Aza is safe. I won't be gone long."

Before she could protest, he pushed open the door and stepped into the yard. He let the door go just as Momma cried, "No, Nathan!"

He crossed the yard in a crouch, the rifle gripped tightly in his hands. The wind pushed at him with angry fingers. The back door was shut. *This is good. Perhaps no one has gone inside.*

He slipped into the house, pulled the door closed, and stood still listening for any sounds. There were none except from the outside. The smell of smoke was strong. The blaze of fires lit the room with an odd glow. Through a window, he could see the village. A strange peace filled the house in contrast to the nightmare outside.

Nathan checked each room. *Clear.* He ran up the stairs. Satisfied everything was in place he returned to the kitchen. He took one last look around and stepped out the door.

As he turned to shut the door, his rifle was jerked from his hand. He froze, his heart pounding, his breath suspended. He felt a pistol jab into his back.

"Well, well. Who do we have here?" asked a deep, raspy voice. "Put your hands behind your head and turn around slowly."

Nathan obeyed. As he turned, he gazed into the piercing eyes of a Cossack soldier.

Chapter 2

The Cossack pointed his revolver at Nathan's head. He looked the boy up and down. His eyes settled on the pistol. Without taking his eyes off Nathan, he backed up two steps, crouched down, and laid the rifle on the ground. "Hand me that pistol," the Cossack commanded, "grip first. No sudden moves."

Nathan obeyed.

The soldier examined it. "An unloaded pistol? Why?"

Nathan didn't respond.

"I asked you a question."

"I didn't have time to load it."

"Where are the balls and powder?"

Nathan pulled back his coat, revealing the bag and powder horn.

"This is a Turkish gun. Where did you get it?"

"My father gave it to me."

"Your father? Where is he?" The soldier's voice was tense.

"He's dead!" Nathan hissed through gritted teeth. Anger burned deep within him. *Why isn't Papa here? He should be here to protect us.*

"I see. So it's a keepsake?" he asked as he slid the pistol in his waist.

Nathan said nothing.

"And is the rifle empty as well?"

"No."

"Ah, you intended to use it against me, no doubt."

Nathan eyed his enemy. *He's older. Maybe fifteen years older than me. About the same height. Fur hat makes him look taller. The ankle-length coat hides his build. His rifle is slung over his shoulder, but his pistol is pointed at me.*

The light flickered across the Cossack's face. He looked grotesque and misshapen. With quick steps, he came so close that Nathan could feel his breath. He felt the pressure of the Cossack's pistol pressing into his belly.

"You're well-armed for a boy. Do you have any other weapons?"

"A knife."

"Where is it?"

"In my boot."

"Which one?"

"My right."

The soldier stepped back. "You're right-handed. Use your left hand and hand it to me, handle first."

Nathan knelt and wrapped his fingers around the knife's handle. *Can I overtake this Cossack?*

Nathan could win a fight with any boy in the village, but he knew he couldn't win against a trained Cossack.

He inched the knife out of its sheath. The Cossack leaned forward, touching the pistol barrel to the top of Nathan's head.

Nathan froze. The hair on his neck stood up. His hand

trembled.

"You wouldn't be thinking of trying something would you, little man? Please don't be foolish. I'd hate to hurt you. Do we understand each other?"

"Yes."

The Cossack backed away, his pistol still aimed at Nathan.

"Lay it on the ground and stand up."

When it was on the ground the two stared at each other for several seconds.

"Now hand it to me," he said cocking his pistol.

Nathan obeyed.

The Cossack looked at the knife. "And this . . . your father's also?

Nathan nodded.

"These weapons make you a threat to me." He shoved the knife into his coat pocket. "Now tell me, where were you going, back to the cellar?"

Nathan didn't respond. *He's been watching me.*

"I was just about to enter your house when I saw you leave the cellar. I decided to wait and see what you were going to do. I suspect there's someone there who waits for your return. Perhaps your mother?"

He knows about Momma! Nathan's shoulders slumped. *What would such a man do to her?* He shuddered at the thought. *Then what—kill her? Kill Israel? Kill me? The old men of the village tell stories of Cossack raids and the things they do.*

Again the woman's scream echoed in his mind.

"Do you have a horse?" the Cossack asked.

"What? Yes." *He's taking my horse? He's taking everything. How can I be a man without a horse?*

"In the barn?"

"Yes."

"Start walking," the Cossack said, waving his pistol toward the barn. After Nathan passed, he bent down and retrieved the rifle.

Nathan glanced toward the village and shivered. Fires sent grotesque shadows flying across the buildings. The acrid taste of the smoke stung his throat. Worst of all, the horrible scream echoed in his mind. *Did this Cossack make her scream? What can I do? He knows where Momma is. I'm trapped. How can I protect her? I can't do anything.*

Nathan pushed open the barn door and spoke to his horse in a soft voice. "It's me, Aza. Don't be afraid."

Aza threw his head back, his eyes wild. "It's all right." Nathan held his hand out, coaxing Aza to come to him. The horse moved forward, nudging Nathan's hand. "That's a good boy," he said rubbing Aza's nose. "It's okay."

"Saddle your horse," commanded the Cossack.

"Are you going to steal him?"

"Why would I steal your horse? I can only ride one at a time."

"Why do you want me to saddle him?"

"You ask too many questions, boy. Just do it."

Nathan reached for a bridle, slipped the noseband over Aza's nose, and placed the bit in his mouth. He pulled the headpiece over Aza's ears and whispered, "It's all right, Aza.

Everything is just fine." *I know you know better.*

Nathan's eyes searched the barn for a way to escape, but there was no way out. He slipped the throat lash under Aza's cheeks and stroked his mane. The horse whinnied as Nathan saddled him. *You know we're going somewhere don't you, boy. So do I, but where?* Taking a last look at the barn, he hoped and prayed there was some way of escape. Something he could do. *Nothing. I can't do a single thing. He has my weapons. He'll shoot me if I try to rush him. I'm trapped.*

The Cossack watched—his pistol didn't waver. "You handle your horse with skill. Can you ride him as well?"

Nathan shrugged his shoulders.

"Never mind, I'll see how good you can ride very soon."

"You're taking me with you? I won't go!"

"You don't have a choice, little man. Ah, yet you do. You can die by my gun. Would you want that? Would you be of benefit to your mother then? Have you forgotten what you've seen this night? What you've heard? You know it's not by accident your house still stands. Nor that your mother is safe in the cellar. She'll have a night and day to think about you—to worry about what has happened to you. We'll return tomorrow night to discuss your ransom with her."

"My ransom? You're kidnapping me?"

"We've wasted enough time. My comrades wait for me." The Cossack grabbed Nathan's arm, pulling him toward the door.

Nathan jerked his arm free. Aza moved back with nervous steps.

"Aha! You're a strong one. You think you're as strong as I am? Don't flatter yourself, little man. I've no more patience. You're my prisoner. Now bring your horse out," said the Cossack as he backed out the door.

"Come, Aza. It's okay, boy."

"My horse is tied to the post in front of your house. Walk your horse there. Don't try anything. My pistol's on you. Now go."

The smoke and fires made Aza skittish. Nathan held the reins tight, spoke to him, and rubbed his nose. At the hitching post, Nathan glanced back at the cellar. *Momma, I should have listened to you. But what difference would it have made? At least you have the house. It could've been your scream I heard.* He shuddered.

"Don't worry about her," said the Cossack. "She'll be all right. Get on your horse, boy. Don't try anything."

Nathan climbed on Aza. The horse relaxed under him.

The Cossack untied his own horse. He mounted, his pistol aimed at Nathan. "We have some distance to cover. Circle around the barn. We'll ride through the woods to the north of the village then turn east to the road going toward the mountains. Ride slow, I don't want to draw anyone's attention. I'll be right behind you with my pistol pointed at your horse. If you try anything, I'll shoot him."

For several minutes they rode through the trees. The firelight flickered on the trees, casting weird shadows all around. Nathan looked from side to side straining to see a friend, someone who might be able to help. It was eerie. The only movement were women mourning over their dead. On the north side of the village, Nathan turned his horse east. They came to the road.

The Cossack nudged his horse beside Nathan's. Without warning, he tossed Nathan's rifle into the air. Nathan snatched it with his left hand and held Aza's reins in the other.

"Good reflexes." The Cossack smiled. "You and your horse make a good team."

Nathan looked away. *He acts as if this is a game.*

"I remember your rifle is loaded. Don't be foolish. Now put your horse to a gallop towards the mountains. I'll see how well you ride."

"Go, Aza!" shouted Nathan as he leaned forward in his saddle. He gripped the reins tightly, and jabbed his heels into Aza's flanks.

The Cossack followed close behind. The glow of the fires disappeared and the wails of the women subsided as the village faded into the night. The only sounds were the horses' hooves pounding the dirt and the cold winter wind. *Run like the wind, Aza. I know this country very well.*

Nathan looked over his shoulder. The Cossack was a horse length behind. *I could go into the woods on my right. By the time he realizes what's happened, I'll be lost in the darkness. If he stops to listen for me he'll lose me. If he follows, the noise of his horse will cover my sounds and I'll lose him. I can circle around the village, stay on the seashore, and go into cliffs. No, I can't! He'll head straight for Momma. What would Papa do? I'm trapped. TRAPPED!*

Chapter 3

When Nathan and the Cossack had galloped about five minutes, the Cossack yelled, "Slow your horse! We're close to the camp now. I can see the fires through the trees."

Nathan pulled back on the reins. "Easy, Aza. Easy, boy." Searching the trees, he saw the fires on their right.

The Cossack said, "Give me your reins".

Nathan hesitated. He shivered as the reality of the situation bore down on him.

"Your reins!" commanded the Cossack as he grabbed them from Nathan's hands. He led Nathan down a narrow path into the camp.

"Nikolai." A voice came through the night. "We thought you had deserted us or some wench had pulled you off into the woods." There was much laughter.

His name is Nikolai.

"You think I'm a fool, eh? You wish my share of the loot would go to you, you pig of a man." More laughter as Nikolai jumped off his horse. "I've a prize. I saw this young one come out of a cellar and I couldn't resist the urge to capture him. I need someone to tend to my horse and shine my boots." He threw back his head and laughed. "He'll make a fine Cossack, no?"

Nikolai pulled Nathan off Aza. There were at least fifty

men in the camp. One of them reached for Aza's reins. Nathan grabbed them first; his eyes flashed with anger. Nikolai stepped between them. "You needn't worry, little man. He'll be rubbed down and fed. You and your horse are both safe here with me."

Shaking with anger, Nathan stared at the ground. "Why should I trust you?" he said under his breath. "You've kidnapped me."

"A fine specimen, Nikolai," thundered an enormous man. He walked up to Nathan and stared down at him with a wide grin. "You have courage, son."

Nathan could not take his eyes off of him. *He must be the leader. He's huge.*

"You have a son now, Nikolai. He is your first. Congratulations."

Nathan wondered at the comment. *A son?*

"Thank you, Commander."

Nikolai pulled Nathan's arm. "Come, sit by the fire and warm yourself. I've a warmer coat and hat for you. A man's coat. A Cossack's coat. You're hungry, no?"

Nathan nodded. He wasn't sure he could find his voice. Several of the men crowded around to get a better look at him.

"Give the lad some room," said Nikolai. He motioned the men back. They didn't hesitate.

He must have authority.

"He's cold and hungry. He needs some good Cossack rations." More laughter. Nikolai disappeared.

Nathan remained by the fire. It felt good. He hoped its warmth would help him to stop shivering. It didn't. He felt many pairs of eyes staring at him.

Nikolai returned with a hat and coat identical to his. He put the hat on Nathan's head and gave it a firm pat to settle it in place. He smiled at the soldiers and winked. "Take off that boy's coat and put on this one." He turned so only Nathan could hear him. "I know you're full of fear," he whispered. "Your world is different now. You have much to learn and see. You'll now get a man's education."

Nathan put on the coat. It was big and heavy. The warmth was instant. He felt different in the Cossack hat and coat. It was strange.

"Sit. I'll get you some fine food."

Nathan sat shivering and waiting. His thoughts raced. *What does he want with me? What does he mean man's education?*

Nikolai brought some bread, cheese, and some kind of hard meat. Nathan hadn't tasted meat like it before. He didn't know how hungry he was until he took the first bite. He ate quickly.

"Look at this appetite!" laughed Nikolai. "You'll be a full grown man in a week at this rate. Come with me. I'll show you your bed."

Nathan followed him to a large tree where Aza was tied.

Nikolai tossed him a woolen blanket and pointed to a place under the tree. "Sleep there. The tree will stop the wind. You'll find the blanket adequate. Sleep well. Tomorrow night we'll visit with your mother, although I suspect nothing will be accomplished with her." He took Nathan's rifle and fired it into the air. He tossed it back to Nathan and winked.

Why does he wink at me? Nathan leaned his rifle against the tree, lay down, and pulled the blanket over him. The camp was noisy, but after a short time, all the men settled on the ground.

Nathan listened to the crackling of the campfire and for the first time since the nightmare started, he cried. Thoughts ran through his mind like a herd of horses. *What does the Cossack want to accomplish with Momma?* It was clear he was Nikolai's property now. He didn't know what that meant, but he knew he would find out. Nathan thought of being home in his bed. Overtaken by exhaustion, he slept and dreamed of Momma, Israel, fires, and screams.

Chapter 4

When Nathan opened his eyes, the sky was the gray of dawn. He sat up and looked around the camp. Most of the men were still asleep, but Nikolai stood by Aza. He was smiling at Nathan. Nathan looked away. *How can this Cossack smile at me after what he's done?*

"Get up, little man. You've had enough sleep. It's time to get up. Come over here."

Nathan stood, wrapped his blanket around his body, and stomped toward Nikolai.

"Where's your rifle?" demanded Nikolai.

Nathan spun, searching around the tree. His rifle wasn't there. He turned back confused.

Nikolai held Nathan's rifle over his head. "Here's your first lesson. Your horse and rifle are most important to you. If you show up in rank without them, for any reason, you'll be flogged to teach you not to forget them again. You'll want to remember this, little man."

Nathan dropped his eyes to the ground.

"Don't look down, boy. Receive instruction like a man. Always look a man in the eye."

Nathan glowered at Nikolai.

"That's it, now let's find you a change of clothes. You're wearing little boy's clothes. You're no longer a little boy.

Follow me."

Nikolai led him to a wagon, searched through the wagon's contents, and found a heavy shirt, woolen pants, socks, a belt, and a pair of boots. He tossed everything except the boots to Nathan. "You must have good boots to protect your feet. Let me know when they start to wear." He tossed them at Nathan's feet. "Change your clothes."

Nathan didn't move.

"Oh, you're a modest man, eh? This is good. Go into the woods over there and change."

Nathan walked toward where Nikolai indicated.

"Wait," Nikolai called.

Nathan turned around.

"Don't try anything stupid, there are guards posted. Not only where you can see, but also where you can't. They know what you think. Don't make it any harder on yourself. Do you understand what I say?"

Nathan nodded. He stomped into the woods and found a large tree that would give him privacy. The clothes were a little large, but not baggy. They were much warmer than his old clothes. He returned to Nikolai.

"They look good on you. Now, throw your old clothes into that fire."

Nathan watched them burn. His eyes watered. Momma had made the shirt for him for his last birthday.

"Are you hungry?"

Nathan shrugged.

"Follow me. It's time to eat some real Cossack food. It'll

make you a man."

Nathan glared at the Cossack, his mind full of fear, anger, and confusion. *Is this real or am I living a nightmare?* He shook his head. He couldn't shake out the thoughts.

"I can see you're worried and tense. You'll get over it. Everything is new to you. You'll adjust soon enough. The food's at that wagon over there." Nikolai nodded toward a different wagon.

Nathan trudged to the wagon Nikolai had indicated.

"Take one of those tin plates. There's some black bread under that cloth. There's stew in the kettle." Nikolai waited for Nathan, and then helped himself. "Let's go into the woods. I'll follow you. I'll let you know how far."

Nathan walked several meters into the woods.

"Hold up, there's a large rock over there," said Nikolai, pointing to their left.

Nathan sat on the rock and dug into the food vigorously.

"Ho, you're hungry! Slow down. There's plenty more where that came from. You'll never have to worry about food as long as you're with me."

Nathan ignored him and continued to wolf down his food.

"You're obstinate, little man. You'll make a fine Cossack."

When they finished, Nikolai said, "I've questions for you. You were born in the village of Gagra, no?"

"Yes."

"Good. You're Russian by birth?"

"Yes."

"And you're a Christian?"

"A Christian? No."

"What then?"

"I'm a Jew," said Nathan proudly.

"A Jew, you say. You won't be when we return to camp."

"How can that be? I was born a Jew. How can I not be a Jew?"

"The fact you're a Jew doesn't matter to me. You're young, healthy, and trainable. This is all that matters. You're going to need a new name. What is your name?"

"Nathan, Nathan Hertzfield."

"Your name will no longer be Nathan Hertzfield." Nikolai thought for a moment. "You're Stepan Ivanov now. Memorize it."

"A new name? You can't change my name just because you decide to!"

"Why do you test my patience, boy? Yes, I can do whatever I decide to do at any time. Now say it."

Nathan hesitated.

"Say it!"

"Stepan . . . I can't do this."

"Do you really think you have a choice, little man? Now say it . . . Stepan Ivanov."

"Stepan Ivanov," spat Nathan. *You can make me say it, but I don't have to accept it. My name is Nathan Hertzfield and it always will be.*

"Good. Now memorize it. This is now your name. We must attend to one other matter."

What else could there be?

"You must make the sign of the cross."

"The sign of the cross? What is that?"

"Watch me!" Nikolai placed the thumb, index, and middle finger of his right hand on his forehead, then moved it to his stomach, then to his right shoulder, and then his left shoulder. "Now you do it."

"What does it mean?"

"It's the recognition of the Father, Son, and Holy Spirit—the belief of all Christians."

"I can't! I won't!"

"At this moment, you're my enemy. You'll do it or I'll kill you!"

"I'd rather be dead," whispered Stepan.

Nikolai ignored the comment. "You don't have to mean it, but you'll have to pretend to be a Christian if you want to stay alive. I'll be asked if you're a Christian. I must say yes. I have to see you make the sign of the cross. Now do it."

With a shaking hand, Stepan duplicated the sign Nikolai had made.

"Excellent. Can you speak any language other than Russian?"

"Yiddish."

"Ah yes, the language of the Jews. I should have known. I've already erased your Jewish nationality. You won't want to speak that language for your own safety. There are many Jews among the Cossacks, but they're not respected. We only tolerate them because we need them. It's better for you if they don't know. Do you understand what I'm saying?"

Stepan nodded.

"Now we have all day in camp. Do you read?" asked Nikolai.

Stepan glared at Nikolai.

"Good. I've some books. It's a good way to pass time. However, if you wish to play one of the games you may do so."

"Books? Games? This is how *the great* Cossacks spend their days?"

"I'll get you a book," said Nikolai laughing. "You're going to make a *great* Cossack. Take your utensils back to the wagon and go to where you slept."

Stepan made a place to sit with his back against the tree. Nikolai tossed a book at Stepan's feet.

Napoleonic Wars? Stepan studied Nikolai's face and thought he saw a trace of a smile. *Is he making fun of me?*

Stepan read until the sun went down pausing only when Nikolai made him eat.

"It's time to go, Stepan," said Nikolai.

"Go where?"

"We have some business to conduct with your mother."

Chapter 5

The full moon lit the countryside. Stepan had always loved the moonlight and how it reflected on the Black Sea, but he didn't that night.

As they approached the village, Stepan pulled Aza to a stop and stared in shock. Several houses were burned to the ground. Smoke floated up from the ash and the wind whisked it away. Some buildings were still upright, but the damage was severe. The bodies on the ground were covered with a sheet or blanket. He saw three bodies in front of the Hebers' house and knew it was his friend David and his parents.

Stepan wept.

Nikolai nudged Aza into movement. They rode up to Momma's house and dismounted. Stepan looked at his house and around the property while Nikolai tethered his horse. Nothing was disturbed. It was out of place compared to the rest of the village, at least what he could see. He looked again at the village. He shook his head in dismay. *Such destruction. How many are dead?*

"Tie up your horse. Let's finish this." Nikolai nodded toward Momma's house.

Nikolai knocked on the door and then made sure Stepan was standing directly in front of it. The door opened slightly and Momma's eyes peered through the opening. Immediately, they widened and she pulled the door open. Tears cascaded down her cheeks. She threw her arms around Stepan and kissed his face numerous times. Then she looked at Nikolai. Her face revealed a mixture of fear and hate. Nikolai looked down at his boots.

She looked at Stepan's clothes. "What is this? Why is he dressed like this? What's your intention with my son?"

"I've brought Stepan to you for a ransom."

Momma's hands flew to her mouth, and her eyes opened wide with disbelief. "Why do you call him Stepan? His name is Nathan, not Stepan."

"Fifty rubles ransom in exchange for your son's freedom."

"Fifty rubles! That's a fortune!" cried Momma. "I don't have that kind of money! How could a widow with two children have that kind of money? You must be . . ." Her words disappeared into thin air. "Even one-tenth of that would be impossible."

"You can't do this!" exclaimed Stepan.

"Quiet, Stepan. This is between your mother and me. Fifty rubles, madam."

"Take my house. It's yours," cried Momma.

"Your house will do me no good. Rubles."

"I cannot."

Nikolai shrugged. "Then it's over."

Momma's shoulders dropped. A resigned expression came over her face.

"Say goodbye to your family, Stepan," Nikolai ordered.

Stepan clenched his fists and looked at Nikolai. *I'm*

Nathan. My name is Nathan. "I won't! This is my family, my home."

"Don't challenge me, little man. Look around you. Do you think I'm not serious? Do you want to risk her safety? Her situation can change."

Stepan slumped in resignation. He breathed a heavy sigh.

Momma circled her arms around him. She whispered in his ear, "Why did he call you Stepan?"

He put his arms around her, squeezed her tightly, and laid his head on her shoulder. They held each other for several minutes. She buried her face in Nathan's coat.

Nikolai cleared his throat.

Momma placed her hands on Nathan's shoulders and held him back at arm's length. Her face was wet with tears. She smiled. "I know you can do nothing about this, Nathan. I can feel the pain in your heart as you can feel mine. I love you, Nathan. Never forget this. I love you with all my heart."

"I love you, Momma."

She let him go, turned, and called Israel from the house. "Nathan's going on a trip," said Momma. "It may be a while before he comes back home."

Israel searched Nathan's face.

"With the Cossack?"

Stepan nodded.

"He forces you to go with him?"

Again Stepan nodded.

"Kidnapper! Murderer!" Israel yelled.

"No, Israel" said Momma. "This will do no good. Don't

make Nathan remember you this way."

Israel started to cry.

Stepan looked at Israel for a long moment.

"My heart breaks also, little brother. You're the man of the house now, Israel. Momma needs you. Be brave. Can you?"

"Y-Yes. I'll do my best. Will you come back, Nathan?"

"I can't lie to you, Israel. I don't know the answer. I'll try."

"You might make a good Cossack when you grow to your brother's size," said Nikolai. "Perhaps Stepan will come back for you someday,"

Israel spat on the ground. "When he does, we'll both come after you."

Stepan looked into Israel's eyes. "I promise I'll come back if possible. If I don't, please know that I love you, little brother." Stepan stepped back and held out his hand to Israel. The brothers shook hands. Then Stepan pulled Israel to him and they hugged. "I love you, Israel," whispered Stepan.

"I love you too, Nathan," sobbed Israel.

"Let's go now," said Nikolai.

Stepan noticed Nikolai had his hand inside his coat and knew he was gripping his pistol.

Stepan plodded to Aza, untied the reins, and stood with his back to the house. He couldn't move nor could he bear to look back.

"Get on your horse, Stepan. It'll be good for you. Now, we'll see how you can really ride that horse. We'll race to the camp."

Stepan stood unmoving.

"Get on your horse, Stepan," demanded Nikolai.

Stepan climbed into his saddle. Before he put his right foot in the stirrup, Nikolai leaned over and smacked Aza on the rump. Aza jumped to a gallop with Stepan trying to get his foot in his stirrup. Nikolai laughed and kicked his horse in the flanks. Stepan was two horse lengths ahead of Nikolai at three kilometers.

"Hold on, Stepan. Hold that big horse back."

Stepan was tempted to ignore Nikolai but thought better of it. A ball in the back wasn't the way he wanted to die. "Whoa, boy! Slow down, big fellow." Stepan stood in the stirrups pulling the reins back hard. Aza came to a jarring halt.

"Ha! What a horse you have Stepan. He's as independent as you." Nikolai reached over, grabbed Aza's reins.

"You do well with a horse," he said with a smile. "Can you shoot as well as you ride?"

"I can hit a bottle at 150 meters."

I'll want to see that," replied Nikolai. "That's as good as our best marksman. What's your name?"

"Na…" He paused, dropping his eyes to the ground.

"Say it," commanded Nikolai.

Stepan looked at Nikolai with tears in his eyes. "Stepan!" he yelled. "My name is Stepan!"

"Again," said Nikolai.

"My name is Stepan."

I've a new name. I'm now considered a Christian. Who am I? What am I? What else is going to happen to me?

Chapter 6

As they walked through the camp, Stepan looked around with apprehension. The camp was alive with activity. Some men were grooming their horses, playing horseshoes, or throwing knives at trees. Others were playing cards, drawing pictures, or reading books. One small group was playing musical instruments. A few were sleeping.

He knew well the trail they took from the village. Escape was on his mind. He surveyed the camp and noted some possible escape routes he could take after dark. *Don't be stupid, Nathan. Where would you go? Not to Gagra. There's no place to go.*

He jumped at Nikolai's voice.

"What're you thinking, little man?"

Stepan ignored the question.

Nikolai leaned toward Stepan and whispered, "Remember your name Stepan Ivanov." He repeated it slower to emphasize the importance, "Step-an I-van-ov."

Stepan felt all eyes on him as Nikolai led him to the food wagon. It seemed everyone stopped their activity to look at him. Stepan didn't make eye contact with anyone.

"Why do they stare at me?" he asked Nikolai.

"You're my first son. Many of them are like you and their memories are at work. They also expect you to try to escape so remember this—we all watch you."

As they walked up to the food wagon, Nikolai said, "Ludvig, meet Stepan. He's hungry enough to eat a horse. See that he's well fed."

Ludvig looked Stepan up and down. "I've no horse meat tonight." He winked at Nikolai. "Maybe tomorrow. Tonight we eat venison. He's skinny. I need to fatten him up. He won't last the month otherwise." He sloshed some stew, beets, cabbage, and a large slice of bread on a tin plate and handed it to Stepan. "Is he old enough for coffee or does he still drink milk?"

"Ask him. He can answer for himself," said Nikolai.

"What'll it be, Stepan?" asked Ludvig.

"Both," said Stepan with resolve.

Ludvig gave him a stern look, and then broke into a boisterous laugh. "I like him, Nikolai. He's his own man. He'll make a fine Cossack, I think."

Stepan blushed.

"He says he can hit a bottle at 150 meters with his rifle," said Nikolai.

"I'd like to see that," said Ludvig with wide eyes. "Such a marksman would be most valuable to me. The men would like to have quail, pheasant, and deer more often. They get tired of beef. They complain, but they don't like to hunt. The only shooting they do is in battle. Perhaps he could be our hunter, Nikolai. What do you think?"

"I suppose he could. We'll know very soon what kind of a marksman he is."

Stepan shrugged his shoulders.

"Perhaps he needs some time to get used to his new surroundings," said Ludvig. "This may be too much for him at the moment."

"Yes," said Nikolai as he studied Stepan. "Perhaps we're rushing him a little."

Nikolai took a plate from Ludvig. "Sit, Stepan," he nodded toward the fire.

Stepan ate with a ferocious appetite. The food was very good. He cleaned up the last few morsels with his bread.

Nikolai said, "You eat like a Cossack, Stepan. You can have more."

"No thank you, it was enough."

"Good. You know when to stop. You have some discipline, I think. Take these plates back to Ludvig and tell him how good the food was. He likes to hear it. He hears many complaints although they aren't meant. He spoils us."

Stepan obeyed and returned. He didn't want to admit it to himself but there was a certain security in staying close to Nikolai.

He didn't have to be told to go to his sleeping place that night. He was exhausted. His mind was full. He concentrated on the night sounds. The fires crackled. The trees made their noises as they resisted the wind. There were quiet conversations with occasional bursts of laughter. The horses snorted and pawed at the snow on the ground. He looked at the moon and stars. His mind returned to Momma and Israel. *I know they're thinking of me. Grieving for me as I am for them. Protect them God . . . and me.*

Chapter 7

Stepan awoke with a start and sprang to his feet.

"Good morning, Stepan," said Nikolai. He had a broad smile on his face and Stepan's blanket dangled from his right hand. "Good reflexes, good balance, but you let me take your blanket." His smile disappeared. "It could have been your rifle again. You'll learn to sleep with one ear tuned and one eye open. You're not home safe in your bed."

Stepan's eyes burned into Nikolai.

"Go get some breakfast. Think about what I said." Nikolai winked, turned, and walked toward the food wagon.

Stepan watched him walk away. *You won't do that to me again.* He grabbed his rifle and followed Nikolai.

"Good morning, Stepan," said Ludvig. "Rest well?"

"Good morning. It wasn't easy to sleep," replied Stepan.

Ludvig chuckled. "It's always that way after a skirmish. Feelings run high and tempers hot. The seasoned fighters harass the new men to keep them stirred up. It's a way of keeping them on edge and ready for more. The wrong look can start a fight. Watch out."

Stepan nodded.

"Don't scare him, Ludvig," said Nikolai as he walked off with a plate of steaming food.

"The coffee's on the fire. It's very strong. There's no more milk. It's a treat after a village raid and doesn't last long."

Stepan poured a cup of coffee. Ludvig handed Stepan a plate full of dark bread and gravy.

Stepan thanked him and turned to find a place to eat.

"There's another one from your village in the camp," said Ludvig.

Stepan turned back sharply his eyes wide with surprise. "Where?"

"I don't know at the moment, but you'll see him. He's a little older than you are. Close to your height I think. I just wanted you to know you're not alone."

"What's his name?"

"I haven't met him. I only know of him."

"Thank you, Ludvig." He turned to walk away. He studied the camp. *Who could it be?*

Nikolai sat under a tree with two other soldiers. He waved Stepan over.

Stepan walked to the three men with measured steps. *Relax, Stepan.*

"Sit," commanded Nikolai. "This is Gustav and Kirill."

Stepan nodded and sat down.

"Gentlemen, this is Stepan. He joined us yesterday."

"Welcome, Stepan," said Kirill, extending a hand.

Stepan paused before taking Kirill's hand. *This isn't a social gathering.*

"He's a shy one," laughed Gustav.

"Give him time," said Nikolai. "He's finding himself. Remember your first day."

"Ah yes, my first day." Gustav's eyes looked somewhere far away.

Stepan ate without words. None were required. The three warriors continued their conversation. He felt invisible except when Nikolai looked his way out of the corner of his eye. *He's watching if I'm paying attention.* Stepan listened with both ears.

"Well, enough of this," said Nikolai. "Come, Stepan. Let's find out what you're to do. No, let's see how you shoot." He started to throw Stepan his leather bag. He hesitated. "Can I trust you, little man?"

Stepan looked at his feet and didn't answer.

"Can I trust you? If I can't, we have a serious problem. I'll not endanger the lives of these men nor, will they allow me to. Have we reached an impasse?"

Stepan met Nikolai's eyes. "I can be trusted."

"Good." He threw the bag to Stepan. "Load your rifle. Let's find some bottles. I want to see you hit them at 150 meters."

"150 meters!" exclaimed Gustav.

"I don't believe it," said Kirill.

"Do you lie to us, Stepan?" asked Nikolai.

"I don't."

"For your sake, you better not," said Nikolai.

"Ask Ludvig for a couple of bottles. No, on second thought, ask him for only one. You might miss the one you're aiming at and hit the one beside it by mistake." Nikolai winked at Stepan.

Stepan turned toward Ludwig's wagon and pretended he didn't see. *Why does he keep winking at me?* Anger filled him quickly when he heard Kirill and Gustav snicker. *You won't laugh at me for long.* He hurried to the wagon.

"I see you're in a hurry, Stepan. Are they putting a burr under your saddle?" asked Ludvig.

Ignoring Ludvig's question, Stepan asked, "Do you have an empty bottle?"

"Big or little?"

"Either. It doesn't matter."

"But of course I do. There are several in the back of the wagon. You choose the size you want. I'll not pick one for you. You know how good you are."

Stepan pulled back the canvas and eyed the bottles. He chose a one-liter bottle.

"A good choice," said Ludvig. "A man who is sure of his eye."

"Did you find one?" called Nikolai.

Stepan held up the bottle.

Nikolai nodded. "You forgot your plate. Come and get it."

Stepan didn't hesitate. He hadn't meant to leave it. *Keep your wits about you, Stepan.* He handed the tin to Ludvig.

"The other one from your village, he's feeding the horses," said Ludvig.

Stepan ran to where the horses were tied. He spotted a man with his back to him. *Vasile! My friend.* As he approached, Vasile turned around. His face was bruised—his left eye swollen. For a moment, Stepan's mouth wouldn't work.

"Nathan!" exclaimed Vasile.

Stepan grimaced. As they hugged, he whispered, "Don't say my name."

"But why?"

"Is this a friend, Stepan?" asked Nikolai.

Stepan jumped. He was unaware of Nikolai's presence. "Uh, yes. This is Vasile."

"Welcome, Vasile." Nikolai reached out his hand.

Vasile glared at him.

"I see. You'll need some time."

"Why'd you call him Stepan?" asked Vasile. "His name is . . ."

"Don't say it," whispered Nikolai.

Vasile glared at Nikolai. "Why?"

"Don't say it unless you want to see your friend dead," whispered Nikolai.

Vasile's eyes narrowed. He grimaced with pain and put his hand to his eye.

"This is neither the time nor the place to discuss this. His name is Stepan. Do you understand?"

Vasile looked at Stepan.

"Do you understand?" asked Nikolai stepping toward Vasile.

"Yes."

"Say his name," demanded Nikolai.

"Stepan."

"Good. I'll give you two a few minutes to talk. Then it will be time for the shoot."

"What shoot?" asked Vasile.

"First things first," said Nikolai. "You have five minutes."

"Come, Vasile," said Stepan. The two friends walked a short distance for privacy.

"What happened to your face?" ask Stepan.

"Aleksandr hit me."

"Who is Aleksandr?"

"My Cossack."

Stepan started to ask why, but Vasile interrupted him. "I don't want to talk about it. Why are you called Stepan?"

"Nikolai changed my name."

"For what reason?"

"Because I'm a Jew. He said Jews aren't liked among the Cossacks and it would be better for me. I'm not to speak of it to anyone. No one else knows."

"I've always known you're a Jew."

"Yes, and I'm asking you as my best friend to keep it to yourself. Promise me you will."

"Of course, Nat . . . I mean Stepan. It'll take some getting used to."

"You must."

"Yes. I understand the importance. I'll remember your old name no more."

"Thank you."

"How did you . . . ?"

"I was kidnapped."

"I, as well. How is your mother?"

"She is as well as can be expected. Yours?"

Vasile's eyes watered. "She's dead."

"No, Vasile!" The woman's scream flooded his mind. "And your father?"

"Dead."

Stepan didn't know what to say. Tears flowed down his cheeks. *This could have been me. Thank you, God.* Stepan groped for words, "I'm so sorry. I can't imagine how painful it is for you."

Vasile wiped his eyes with the back of his hand. "We must stick together, Stepan. And protect each other. You're like a brother to me. Your momma is like my mother."

"Yes, I feel the same." He hugged Vasile.

The sounds of Nikolai's boots broke up their conversation.

"It's good to see two friends reunited. I've just the thing for you, Vasile. Stepan was just about to show us what a marksman he is. He tells us he can hit a target at 150 meters. What do you think of that?"

"I think he's being modest. He can do better than that."

"You're joking. You know such to be a fact? You have witnessed this?"

"Many times. We are . . . were the village hunters."

"But, you're older. Is he as good as you?"

"Better. Much better."

Nikolai's mouth curled into a smile. "I can see a deer at that distance, but a bottle?" Then his eyes narrowed. "And a man? How far?" He turned and searched Stepan's eyes.

I can't shoot a man. Never could I shoot a man. Not at any distance.

"Come, let's get this event underway," said Nikolai. "Do you have a rifle, Vasile?"

"No. It was lost in the fire."

"We have several. We'll find you one. Who's your Cossack?"

"Aleksandr."

"Ah . . . he's a tough one. Now I understand why your face is bruised. You'll not want to test him. He has no patience," warned Nikolai.

Stepan saw fear in Vasile's eyes for a split second.

"Let's do this shooting. Come," said Nikolai.

Stepan and Vasile followed Nikolai to the supply wagon.

"Gustav, this is Vasile, Stepan's friend. He's a hunter as well. Will you find him a rifle? No ammunition. The day is passing us by. We'll go into the woods and find a suitable place. Bring the rifle and find us. You do want to witness this, don't you?"

"But of course. Two hunters." Gustav walked away, shaking his head.

"Come," said Nikolai. He jerked his head toward the trees. "We must find a place for this shooting demonstration."

Chapter 8

Nikolai sent Kirill to find a location where Stepan could demonstrate his shooting. It was nearly forty minutes before he returned.

"There's a spot along the ridge," Kirill said excitedly.

"Good," said Nikolai. Turning to Stepan he asked, "Do you have everything you need in your bag?"

"Yes."

"Then let's go. I have the bottle."

Kirill led Stepan, Nikolai, and Vasile into the woods. Ludvig had been watching. Taking off his apron, he followed.

When they arrived at the place, Nikolai tossed the bottle to Kirill. "Measure the distance, 150 meters, and set up the bottle." Kirill started pacing off the distance.

"Well, Stepan, the moment of truth has arrived," said Nikolai.

Stepan ignored the comment. A slight breeze blew past him. Glancing up, he watched the movement of the branches and then looked toward the sea. There was nothing more than the normal ebb and flow against the shore. *Good. This'll make it easier.*

"You haven't a thing to say?" asked Nikolai.

"My shooting will speak for me."

"Ah! A man of confidence. I'll be close by if you need me."

Nikolai walked a few meters away and leaned against a tree.

Stepan wondered why he would need Nikolai. He looked toward Vasile, who smiled and winked.

Stepan winked and smiled back. Placing his rifle between his knees, he opened his hunting bag. A noise behind made him jump. Turning, he was surprised to see Ludvig along with what looked to be the entire camp walking out of the woods. His hands shook.

Vasile stepped close to Stepan. "Don't worry. You've shot in front of an audience many times. Pretend you're back in the village."

Stepan relaxed. Closing his eyes he imagined he was back in Gagra. All his friends were there. Smiling to himself, he turned his attention back to his rifle. It was unloaded and working properly. Pulling the hammer back halfway, he examined the nipple. *Clean.* Wiping his forehead, he checked the wind. He poured some powder into his hand. *Dry.* Using a brass measure, he scooped it up, transferring it to the barrel. He pulled a cloth patch from his pouch, placed it over the end of the barrel, and put a lead ball on it. He trimmed the excess cloth and rammed the patch and ball down the barrel. The mark on the ramrod showed they were solidly placed.

"How're you feeling?" asked Vasile.

"A little nervous."

"You can do this. You've made more difficult shots."

"I know, but it's not the same." A bead of sweat rolled down his nose and dripped onto his hand.

"You won't miss. Now focus on our village."

Stepan turned his thoughts back to the village.

Kirill returned. "It's on a boulder, about a meter off the ground." He pointed.

Stepan followed Krill's finger and saw his target.

Nikolai stepped close to Stepan. "This is the moment of truth, little man. Are you ready to show us what a marksman you are?"

Stepan nodded. He tilted his head back. Closing his eyes, he felt the sun. The breeze cooled his face. He drew three deep breaths. *Relax.* The water lapped the shore, the birds sang, and the branches rustled. There were no other sounds. Slowly opening his eyes, he let them find his target.

He reached in his bag. His fingers found a percussion cap. He fixed the cap on the nipple. A young White Birch tree grew to his right. He placed the barrel in a fork of the tree that was chin high. He positioned the barrel, balanced the gun, and set the butt of the rifle against his right shoulder. He settled his feet and dug the soles of his boots into the dirt. He looked again to find his target. Slowly, he cocked the hammer. Closing his eyes, he whispered, "God, help me."

He took a deep breath, looked down the long barrel across the sight, and found his mark. His right eye focused on the bottle. The barrel moved slightly above and to the right of the object. Closing his left eye, he checked the sight. He took a deep breath, held it, and slowly squeezed the trigger.

The gun roared, the bottle disintegrated, and the men's cheers filled the air.

"Thank you, God," he whispered.

He brought the rifle to half cock, removed what was left of the cap, and blew through the vent of the nipple. Then he wiped down the barrel. Looking at Vasile, he smiled. Nikolai stepped forward and slapped him on the back.

"Not bad," said Nikolai. Shaking his head, he repeated, "Not bad."

Chapter 9

The day after the shooting Stepan and Vasile were assigned to the hunting team along with two others. Stepan knew the others were to make sure he and Vasile didn't escape.

After two weeks, they were allowed to hunt alone. Often, Stepan noticed that Vasile had bruises, but he wouldn't ever talk about it. When they returned each day, their bags were full of quail, pheasant, and small game. They left the deer and elk where they lay after the kill. There was no trouble getting volunteers to bring them in to camp. In the evenings, Stepan and Vasile compared notes. They never talked about family, it was too painful.

One morning, Nikolai approached Stepan after breakfast. "You've done well, little man. Now, it's time to start learning about being a Cossack."

Stepan said nothing.

"You'll still hunt, at least for a while, but there's much you need to know." He handed Stepan a rifle.

"What's this for?"

"You can't use your hunting rifle except for hunting," said Nikolai.

"Why?"

"For several reasons—the main one being, it won't carry

a bayonet."

"I'll have a sword, won't I?"

"Yes, but it's for a different situation—when you're fighting on horseback or when you can't use your rifle.

"I don't understand."

"Your rifle is of no value if you're on horseback unless you use it as a club. If you're in close quarters, you won't be able to swing it. Your pistol is practical, but you'll only have one shot."

"I don't have a pistol. You took it from me."

Nikolai pulled Stepan's pistol from his pocket and handed it to him.

Stepan looked at the pistol for a moment and then at Nikolai. A hint of a smile tugged at Stepan's mouth, but he caught himself and pushed the pistol into his belt. He wondered why Nikolai had decided to trust him now.

"Your sword is your most important weapon, in that situation—on horseback, in close quarters—because of its reach. However, it takes a strong arm and hand to swing it with any accuracy. I'll teach you how to use it, but you'll need to strengthen your muscles. If you find yourself in hand-to-hand combat, you'll need this as well." He held Stepan's knife in his hand. "I believe this is yours." He smiled at Stepan.

Surprised, Stepan took the knife, quickly looked down, and shoved it into his right boot. "Thank you," he said quietly.

Nikolai winked. "You've earned my trust, little man."

Stepan nodded.

"I know you haven't thought about this kind of fighting. You may not experience it soon, but it's imperative to know. I'll teach you how to defend yourself. You may find yourself in a life-and-death situation."

Shaking his head, Stepan walked away.

Nikolai grabbed his arm. "This is difficult for you, but these are things you need to know. You need to trust me. I'm your best friend."

Stepan jerked his arm free and walked into the woods. His mind full of confusion, he walked for nearly an hour trying to come to grips with the inevitable. Turning to go back to the camp, he was startled to see Nikolai about thirty meters in front of him, leaning against a tree.

Nikolai waited for Stepan to approach him. "This is hard to accept, but you must. You're not alone. I'm not the only one who has an interest in you. There's Ludvig, Vasile, and others.

"Who?"

"Several. Your shooting demonstration has brought you into the camp more quickly than usual."

"What does that mean?"

"It means you've been accepted and you've earned the respect of most. Oh, there are a few who're jealous and see you as a threat, but they still respect you. They see your value in providing meat and they know you'll learn to be a Cossack. It's just a matter of time. You can count on them to come to your aid if they're needed."

Stepan looked up at the sky. *God help me. I'll never become one of them.* He walked back to the camp. If Nikolai said anything else, the words escaped him. He heard Nikolai's steps for a short distance and then there were only the sounds of the night.

Back at the camp he lay down, pulled a blanket over his head, and slept. No one bothered him. They'd seen this many times. Only Nikolai, Ludvig, and Vasile kept a watch over him.

For the next several days Nikolai taught Stepan how to use his sword and bayonet. Stepan finally resigned himself to the training. He and Vasile competed with each other and compared the tactics of Nikolai and Aleksandr.

"Which do you think is the better?" asked Vasile.

Shaking his head, Stepan said, "I don't want to fight either one in a life-and-death skirmish."

Vasile agreed.

"I'm jealous," confessed Vasile after Stepan went on one scouting trip with Nikolai, as an observer, and on a second trip to help appropriate supplies. "Aleksandr says I've more to learn before he'll let me go with him."

"I wonder why. Nikolai says this is the perfect time for me to go with him. The Commander is sending out small scouting parties—only six men at a time to see if there are any signs of Turks. He says it's less threatening to the villagers and more successful for obtaining supplies. Nikolai has told me that our village wasn't supposed to be a raid. They were scouting for Turks. Now they've finished and they're ready to head back home. Besides, the Commander doesn't want to lose any more men or have more wounded to worry about."

"You're lucky to have Nikolai as your Cossack."

Stepan didn't respond.

"Stepan?" Vasile began.

"What?"

"Do you know how close we've been to Gagra all this time?"

"Yes. It's strange being this close to home and yet so far away."

"Have you thought about . . . "

"Of course, many times, but it would be foolish. The minute they knew we were missing, they'd head straight to the village, and my house. Do you think they haven't been expecting us to try?"

"I know you're right. Besides, there's nothing there for me now."

"Then put it out of your mind." In spite of himself, Stepan was becoming a Cossack.

Several nights later, Stepan had just finished his supper and was talking with Ludvig. Nikolai walked up and slapped Stepan on his back.

"Let's go fishing, Stepan," said Nikolai, handing him a pole.

Stepan didn't have to be asked twice. He loved to fish. He took the pole and the two walked to a wide stream. After baiting their hooks, they sat and watched their lines.

"Tell me about the Cossacks," said Stepan. "If I have to be a Cossack, I think I should know who they are. Where did they come from?"

"*If* you have to be Cossack? You are one."

"Then what's my history?"

Nikolai stared at the water. "Well, we go back nearly eight hundred years to 1100."

"Eight hundred years?"

"Yes. We have a lot of history. We have guarded Russia from her enemies many of those years. We're considered heroes."

"For raiding villages, raping, stealing, and killing?"

"No. That happens. We're heroes for guarding the borders of Russia and protecting her possessions. We're only one of many divisions of Cossacks. We have a hetman and an *Okrug Ataman* who lead us and speak for us."

"I don't understand."

"Our hetman is our main leader, second to the tsar. He negotiates with the tsar—he makes an exchange of our protection for, what shall I say, uh . . . wages. We have a council meeting, discuss the terms, and we decide if we're going to accept or not. For example, we received our own land to farm and build on in exchange for our loyalty to the tsar. We are not serfs. We own the land and we can sell it if we want. We also have an *Okrug Ataman* who oversees our community."

"*Okrug Ataman*?"

"Yes. *Okrug* means territory or district. *Ataman* means leader. There are many leaders under the hetman and the Okrug Ataman is assigned a territory to manage. We live on the Don River and we're Don Cossacks."

"Why did the Cossacks come to Gagra?"

"Do you remember the raid on Gagra by the Turks several years ago? The Don Cossacks had been fighting those Turks in the mountains. Your village was on the way when the Turks came down from the mountains. The Don Cossacks pursued them into your village, overtook them, and pushed them farther south."

"What about now?"

"In exchange for our help, the Georgians agreed to pledge allegiance to the Russians. They knew if they didn't, we would leave and the Turks would come back and destroy their villages. By submitting, they would continue to have the protection of Russia."

"But I've heard some of the Cossacks talk against Russia."

"Yes, some do. We're really freemen."

"What does freemen mean?"

"It means we're free. We Cossacks are really freemen, not bound by any country, any land. We fight for Russia now, but there are times we give our allegiance elsewhere. We're free to choose."

"This is why you're Russians?"

"We're not Russians. We're freemen. In exchange for land along the Don River, we agreed to become Russian soldiers."

"Then you're no longer freemen."

"We're freemen. We can decide at any time to leave the Russian Army and join another or no other."

"Would you lose the land?"

"No," laughed Nikolai. "That land will be ours forever . . . our children's."

"Do you have such land?"

"Yes. Land and a home."

"Do you have children?"

Nikolai looked away. "No."

"Then who would get your land?"

Nikolai looked at Stepan and shrugged. "Many of the men have families there. Some have offered to buy it."

"If they have families, why do they leave their homes for such a long period?"

"We're Cossacks. We live on our horses. Horses are our life. Most of our horses have been trained since birth. We even compare the beauty of a woman to the beauty of a horse. We must always take good care of our horses."

"I take good care of my horse."

"Yes, but you don't know how to train one for battle. When you no longer have Aza, you'll learn the difference between a hunting horse and a war horse. Or do you think you'll have Aza forever?"

Stepan didn't respond.

"You need to be prepared for the possibility of Aza being killed in battle or breaking a leg or becoming fatally ill. All these things are possible."

"I don't want to think about it."

"That may be, but think about it you must."

Changing the subject, Stepan asked, "Why did you attack Gagra?"

"We didn't attack Gagra. We needed food and horses, we were fired on, we reacted."

"Who fired on you?"

"Who's to know? It was dark."

"But you could have . . ."

"We could've what? For all we knew, it was Turks."

"But the women . . . the children . . ."

"You think women and children cannot fire a gun? Use a knife? Were you not carrying a rifle when I stopped you? Did you not have a pistol? A blade? What if I hadn't stopped you? Would you have killed me?"

Stepan was quiet.

"Not all battles are intended, Stepan. The villagers probably thought we were Turks."

"You don't look like Turks."

"Have you ever seen a Turk?"

"No."

"Then how do you know? There was no moon, they fired, it happened."

"Do you expect villagers to simply give up their horses, their food?"

"They're Russian citizens who need protecting. We're Russians chasing Turks out of Georgia. It seems a reasonable exchange, does it not?" questioned Nikolai.

"Yes and no."

"Yes and yes."

"Are you going back to Russia now?"

"It's up to the Commander. We've seen no Turks in Georgia this trip. We're tired and want to go back home and live in peace. We're a peaceful people."

"Not from my perspective," said Stepan.

"You'll change your perspective."

"Why did you kidnap me?"

"We lose men, we recruit men."

"By kidnapping them?"

"You can tell me a better way? Would you have come if I'd asked you to? Should I've asked your Momma for permission?"

"But you tried to ransom me."

"It was fair. I gave her a choice. If she had paid the ransom, we could have bought horses, food, and weapons. Sometimes this happens. It's a fair trade. In your case, it didn't work out."

"She's a widow."

"Did I know that? Don't blame me for her circumstances. She has another son. She has her home. I was fair."

Stepan had no more words and no more questions.

Chapter 10

Two nights later the Commander addressed his men.

"We've buried our dead. Our wounded are rested. The weather is favorable and it's time to go home. We leave at first light in the morning."

A loud cheer filled the air.

Nikolai slapped Stepan on the back and laughed. "We're going home."

I'm not going home.

When it quieted down, the Commander said, "Ludvig has prepared a special meal this evening, potato varenyky and cabbage borshch. Enjoy."

Another cheer filled the air. The camp was transformed. Everyone was in a party mood. Everybody seemed to be relaxed and friendly.

"Let's get some of this food before it's gone," coaxed Nikolai.

They got their plates and found a quiet place on the rocks.

"Good food, eh?" Nikolai asked Stepan.

"Yes. Ludvig is a good cook."

"That he is. You should taste his cooking when we're home—when he has all the seasonings, meats, and vegetables. It's something for you to look forward to."

"Look forward to? It's not my home. My home is behind

us."

"Your home *was* behind us. No longer. You're headed home now."

There was silence between the two for a while. Nikolai stood. "Do you want me to get you some more, Stepan?"

"No. I'm full."

"So am I," said Nikolai, patting his stomach. "Give me your plate, I'll take it back."

Stepan handed Nikolai his plate.

"I'll be back in a moment," said Nikolai.

I'm headed home? Stepan walked away from the camp. He looked in the direction of Gagra. In his mind he could see the village, his home. He strained his eyes to see the village, but there was only darkness. *What are Momma and Israel doing? Probably preparing to go to bed. Are they thinking of me?*

Nikolai walked up behind him. "It's out there, Stepan. Your past."

My past.

A gust of bitter wind whipped at them.

"Come, let's get close to the fire," urged Nikolai. "This wind will turn us into icicles. Some hot coffee will take the chill off."

Stepan followed Nikolai to the fire.

Nikolai poured two tins of coffee, handed one to Stepan, and sat down. The camp was quieting down. No one else was around this fire.

"Tell me about your father, Stepan."

"My father?" Stepan asked, staring into the fire.

"Yes. What was he like?"

Stepan was quiet. *Why is he asking me this?*

"How old were you when he died?"

"Fifteen," Stepan sighed, "My father built things and hunted. He taught me what he knew. He taught me how to ride. Aza belonged to him.

"What happened to him?"

"Why do you want to know?" Stepan demanded.

"It's all right if you don't want to tell me."

The two men sat in silence sipping coffee. The fire crackled while the smoke curled into the air until the wind whipped it away.

Stepan blinked several times and cleared his throat. "He was helping rebuild a house that was destroyed during the Turkish raid. A wall collapsed and fell on him. He was crushed. He didn't have a chance to tell me good-bye."

"That's a tragedy. He sounds like he was a good father."

"He was."

"So you became the man of the house and the hunter?"

"Yes."

"School?" quizzed Nikolai.

"Momma taught me."

"She must be very smart."

"Yes." Stepan stared deep into the black of the night visualizing, Momma. "She is."

Nikolai let Stepan have the moment. Then he asked, "And you're angry at him?"

Stepan sighed. "Not at him, just angry."

"And you're angry with me also?" Nikolai asked with a gentle voice.

Stepan, surprised by the question, turned quickly toward Nikolai, his hands trembling. Glaring at Nikolai, he spat, "Yes! It was cruel of you to take me from Momma."

"It's good for you to be honest. I can see you're angry and releasing it will free your heart."

Stepan did feel a strange sense of release as the emotion flowed from him.

"And you hate me?"

"Yes, I hate you." Stepan admitted.

Nikolai stood. "I'll leave you to your thoughts," he said softly and walked to his bed.

Stepan stared into space for several minutes. Anger raged within him. His thoughts tumbled over everything that happened during the night his world changed.

Stepan had never been this far into the mountains. On the third day, Stepan stopped Aza and stared behind them. It was almost dark. *I'm tired. I hope we stop for the night soon.* The trail was narrow and rugged. He was near the front of the regiment with Nikolai, Vasile, and Aleksandr. The Commander led the column. As they rounded a ridge, a shot rang out. The Commander slumped in his saddle.

"Get the Commander!" yelled Nikolai.

Two men tried to pull him to safety. One fell from a shot to the head. The other dragged the Commander behind a rock.

“I can’t see them!” shouted Aleksandr. Another shot rang out and Aleksandr’s horse went down. Aleksandr took cover behind his horse.

Stepan pulled his pistol from his belt—his eyes darting wildly. *Where are they? I can’t see them.*

“Move back, Stepan,” commanded Nikolai.

Another shot split the air and Vasile cried out. His right arm fell to his side, dripping blood down his hand and fingers. His horse reared and he fell to the ground.

Nikolai jumped from his horse and pulled Vasile to cover.

In that instant, Stepan saw a man rise up with his rifle aimed toward him. There was a flash and a lead ball ricocheted off a boulder to the right of Stepan’s head. Pieces of rock pelted the side of his face. Aza moved crazily under him. “Steady, Aza,” urged Stepan.

The man disappeared.

Stepan slipped off Aza, keeping his eyes directed at the spot. At that instant, another man to the right raised up. Stepan cocked the hammer, aimed, and fired. The man’s head jerked back in an odd way, his body slammed back against a rock, and he pitched forward unmoving.

Aza, startled at the blast, jerked sideways and pushed Stepan into a rock. Stepan fell to the ground unconscious.

Chapter 11

"Stepan, Stepan."

In the distance, Stepan heard Nikolai call his name. It was completely dark and quiet, except for Nikolai's voice.

"It's over, Stepan."

Stepan opened his eyes. Nikolai leaned over him. Stepan was lying on a blanket—a wet cloth across his forehead. Reality roared back into his mind.

"Where am I?"

"In camp."

"The Commander . . . is he?"

"He's all right. A wound to his side probably broke some ribs, but the ball is out."

"Vasile?"

"A wound and broken arm. He'll heal."

Stepan's face clouded. "I killed a man! I can't believe it." *Maybe I really am a Cossack now.*

"You defended yourself. He was going to shoot you."

The scene replayed in Stepan's head. He saw the whole battle.

"Do you remember?"

"Yes . . . vividly. I can see his face. It's horrible. He looks so awful with blood spurting from his head."

"Then you remember that you were in danger?"

"Yes, but I'm so confused. I was excited. Why would I be excited, Nikolai? It was horrible. I killed him." Stepan stammered.

"Who's to understand emotions in battle? Maybe because you saved yourself. Perhaps because it was a good shot. It was better him than you. Don't you agree?"

"I wish it were neither."

"You can't undo it, Stepan. Is it better him than you?"

"I'm not sure."

"He was a Turk, an enemy. He was headed toward your village."

"How do you know that?"

"The trail we're taking from Gagra, they were taking to Gagra."

"How were we surprised? We sent scouts ahead of us."

"We found our scouts in the rocks—their throats cut. The Turks knew we were coming and set up an ambush. Stepan, you must think about this. Your conclusion will free you or destroy you."

"How?"

"If you think it was you who should have died, you'll carry a death wish with you into every skirmish. You'll place yourself in harm's way hoping for an end to your nightmare. And you'll endanger others, too."

Stepan stared past Nikolai to some invisible, faraway place.

Nikolai continued, "If you conclude you were defending yourself, you'll be able to let go and live. It won't be immediate but it'll happen. I know this from experience."

"I'm not so sure."

"Then you're a dead man. It happened, you can't change it. If you don't see the truth, you'll never forgive yourself. Ask yourself why you shot him. Therein lies your freedom.

"Have you ever killed anyone?"

"Yes, but like you, I've never killed except in self-defense," whispered Nikolai. "I've left the brutality to those of a darker nature. I've been as loud as the others, taken my share of the spoil, and let the others assume what they wanted about me. I've denied no accusations. Let them think of me what they want."

"You've fooled them all this time?"

"It's not a matter of fooling anyone. What do you remember of this incident other than what involved you directly?"

Stepan thought for a moment. "Nothing."

"This is what I mean. There was so much happening. One can only be aware of what directly affected him. There were no enemies left alive. We killed many men. Each man lives with his nightmare, just as you're living with yours."

Stepan shuddered.

"Remember this, Stepan, and learn from it. It's the only way to have peace in this madness."

I killed a man. I killed a man. How could I do such a thing?

Stepan turned away. Tears ran down his face soaking his blanket. He sobbed until his body was too exhausted for any more tears.

From that moment on, Stepan was treated differently by Nikolai, Vasile, and the other Cossacks, Stepan was no longer treated like a boy; he was now considered a man. He was a Cossack, not in just Nikolai's eyes, but in the eyes of the Commander as well. The Commander's flesh wound was healing. He made it a point to acknowledge Stepan often.

Vasile shadowed Stepan everywhere.

"You sure showed them, Stepan."

"Showed them what?"

"That you're a Cossack. Even Aleksandr treats me better because you and I are friends."

Stepan was confused by his own mixed emotions. He enjoyed the respect, but how he attained it bothered him.

A week later, the Commander gave the order to move on. Scouts were sent ahead and reported back that there were no signs of Turks. The Commander wanted to be back in the community by spring to plant crops for the winter food supply.

Chapter 12

The winds blew stronger and colder. At night, the regiment spread out in the rocks to find shelter from the brutal weather. They climbed farther up the mountains until the snow obliterated their vision. Stepan had only seen this snow from his village. It always looked so beautiful from a long distance, but here the winds were bitter and the snow was swirling fiercely.

"Is it always this ferocious, Nikolai?" shouted Stepan, trying to be heard over the howling wind. He pulled his head deeper into his wool coat and tilted his head down. "I can barely see."

"Only where the wind is forced through a pass like this," Nikolai shouted back. "Be grateful we don't have to face an enemy in this. We shouldn't be in this passageway long."

Stepan leaned forward, talking into Aza's ear—encouraging him to be calm and patting him on his neck. Then as if a giant hand cleansed the air, the blowing snow disappeared. The wind was still strong, but they were in the open, with the sun shining brightly. Stepan's breath caught at the splendor of the scene before him. *These mountains are so beautiful—rugged and magnificent.* His eyes widened to take in a valley with another wall of rock behind it.

"Nikolai, how long will we be in the mountains?"

"About six weeks if we don't get snowed in. February is the worst month. We arrive in March."

The days went by surprisingly fast. As Nikolai had said, February was brutal. They had to shelter in a temporary camp in a ravine. Trees were scarce. The Commander didn't allow any of the men to go very far to find and cut firewood for fear they'd be lost. A few horses didn't survive, but due to the Commander's wisdom they had enough spares so none of the men had to walk. Stepan thought walking might have been faster at times.

February turned into March.

Are we ever going to get out of these mountains? Stepan eased Aza down a rocky crag on the south side of a ridge. As the makeshift trail curved around to the north, a wide vista opened before his eyes. It was a clear day and Stepan could see for what seemed like forever. The view captivated him. He pulled Aza to a halt and stared at the artistry of creation.

"Beautiful, isn't it?" asked Nikolai.

Stepan watched a hawk flying far below them. Its wings spread level; it spiraled down riding the air current. Stepan's eyes followed it until the hawk disappeared behind a cliff.

"Is that Russia?"

"Yes," smiled Nikolai.

Stepan noted a hint of pride in his response. "Where are we going?"

"Do you see that body of water?" Nikolai pointed to the northwest.

"The one that looks like a small Black Sea?"

"Yes. That's the Sea of Azov. The Don River flows into its east end." Nikolai indicated with his finger.

Aza raised his head and snorted. Stepan shifted in his saddle and stood in his stirrups to get a better look. His eyes followed Nikolai's finger.

"Follow the river north to where it bends west—where it bends back to the north, on the west bank, lies Aksay, our settlement. Have you heard these names?"

"Momma taught me about the seas, rivers, and major cities. I don't recall Aksay."

"It's a beautiful settlement of a few thousand people. There are rolling hills of fertile land that produce a large variety of crops. The river gives a steady supply of water. It's beautiful country. You can almost smell it from here."

Stepan took a deep breath. "I smell the pine trees."

Nikolai laughed. "Once you've been there, you'll know what I mean."

"What kind of crops do you grow on your land?"

"I don't grow crops. I've less than an acre. I'm a teacher of military tactics."

Stepan stared at Nikolai suspiciously. "A teacher? You don't look like a teacher."

"And what does a teacher look like?"

"I don't know," laughed Stepan.

Nikolai looked at Stepan with a wide grin.

"What are you smiling about?" asked Stepan.

"You. This is the first time I've ever heard you laugh."

I did laugh!

Nikolai tilted his head back and laughed with gusto. Stepan laughed as well.

The two men became silent. Stepan was amazed at himself. *I'm laughing. It feels good.*

Confused, Stepan turned away. Looking into Russia, he searched his soul. *I want to hate you, Nikolai. I try to hate you.* He wasn't aware of Nikolai or anything else for several minutes. Stepan blinked back a tear. He realized that Nikolai was becoming like a father to him. Guilt flooded him. *How can I feel this way about him? He took me from my mother. He kidnapped me! He's not my father!*

Stepan prodded Aza and started down the trail.

Nikolai let him go.

Chapter 13

In the middle of March they entered Aksay. Townspeople stood alongside the road waving flags of white, blue, and red, as they shouted and laughed. Soon they were surrounded by the citizens of Aksay.

Women hurried from their houses, loading food and drinks on tables set up along the street. Stepan felt something shoved into his hand. He looked down at a chunk of black bread. He tried to see who had placed it there, but there was a sea of smiling and laughing faces. He nodded and took a bite. The burst of applause at his acceptance of their gift surprised him.

The transformation of the Cossacks was amazing. They turned from hardened fighters to family men before Stepan's eyes. He caught a glance of Aleksandr embracing a woman and then bending over to scoop up two beaming children.

"What do you think, Stepan?" shouted Nikolai, trying to be heard over the crowd.

"It's wonderful."

"Welcome home. We might as well climb down. We won't be able to travel any farther on horseback."

Stepan climbed off Aza. As soon as he did, there was a crowd of people around him, slapping him on the back, shaking his hand. Women kissed him. Stepan felt his face turn warm. He knew he was blushing, which made the girls pursue him even more.

He looked for help, but Nikolai was caught up in another crowd. He winked at Stepan. This time, Stepan winked back. He heard someone calling his name. *Was that Vasile?* Stepan tried to see who it was, but was swept away in a sea of jubilation.

Late into the night, the festivities finally starting to slow down, Nikolai found Stepan. "How are you, little man?"

It's been a long time since he called me that. "I'm not sure," replied Stepan. "I've been hugged and kissed so many times, I feel like my ribs are broken and my face is sore. They don't even know me."

"This is true, but they understand and accept you as one of us. You're not the first new face they've seen. They know how we replenish our losses."

Emotion flowed over Stepan like a river. "But what about . . ."

"The dead?" asked Nikolai softly.

"Yes," Stepan replied, looking down at his boots.

"That reality has already come to those families. When they saw their Cossack wasn't among us, they moved off quietly to their dwelling and mourned. It's the custom of our people to rejoice for those who've returned and then mourn with those who've lost a Cossack. The news will travel through the community quickly, and tomorrow evening there'll be a memorial for those who were lost."

"This is hard to grasp," said Stepan.

"It's our way. I think we can go to the house now."

"Where are our horses?"

"They're in the stable. They've been well taken care of. I suspect Aza has a girlfriend by now. We'll get them in the morning. Come, I live a little way down this road."

The two men walked about four hundred meters to a small house.

"Here it is," said Nikolai.

Stepan stood looking at the house. It was too dark to see it well.

"You'll see it in the morning. If you're as tired as I am, you don't want to stand any longer."

"I'm exhausted," replied Stepan. "I think the journey, everything, is weighing me down."

He followed Nikolai into the house.

Nikolai lit a lamp. "Here's my castle."

Stepan looked around the room. It was comfortable with two chairs, a desk, and to his amazement, a bookshelf full of books. *I never suspected this.*

Nikolai showed Stepan the rest of the house—a cooking area and two bedrooms. "What do you think?" asked Nikolai.

"It's very nice. It's more than I expected. And you live here by yourself?"

"I do. This room is for visitors. It's yours." Nikolai extended his hand toward the room.

Stepan walked in slowly with Nikolai behind him, holding the lamp. There was a bed, chair, desk, washstand with a bowl, some hooks with a sleeping robe, and another bookcase filled with books. Stepan was amazed.

"Well? Do you like it?"

"I'm overwhelmed," said Stepan, "but yes."

"Good," said Nikolai as he slapped Stepan on the back. "You can wash up there. I think that robe will fit you. I'll see you in the morning."

"Good night, Nikolai, and thank you."

Nikolai set the lamp on a stand by the bed. "You're welcome." He disappeared out the door.

Stepan undressed, washed, and fell into bed. He stared at the ceiling with a smile on his face and let sleep take him away.

Chapter 14

The next morning Stepan awoke to the delicious smell of coffee, bread, gravy, and something he couldn't identify. Rubbing his eyes, he sat up on the edge of the bed. He stretched, releasing the sleep from his body. *No clean clothes.* He slipped on a robe, cinched it tight, and walked into the kitchen.

"Good morning, Stepan, or should I call you sleepy head? I thought these smells would wake you up. Help yourself to the coffee, bread, bacon, and cheese. The eggs are almost done."

Bacon! I can't eat bacon. He frowned at the table.

"What's wrong, Stepan?"

"I . . . I can't eat bacon. It's from hogs."

"Why not? It's fresh, right off the farm—a gift from Ludvig—well aged and begging us to eat it. "

"I just can't, Nikolai. I'm a Jew."

Nikolai tilted his head back and groaned. Shaking his head, he said, "No, you're not, Stepan. You're a Russian Cossack soldier and an Orthodox Christian."

"Only because you say so. Not in my heart."

"This may be so, Stepan, but it's going to be very costly for you. We Russians love our bacon, ham, pork chops, and especially smoked pork cooked slowly over an open spit.

Besides, are you sure you want to make this revelation every time you're in this position? What you eat or don't eat in this house is of no matter to me, but outside . . . I think you'll want to think about this seriously. Besides, you'll lose a lot of weight," Nikolai smiled.

Stepan stared at the bacon as if it were his enemy.

"Is your God a forgiving God, or will he strike you with lightning if you eat pork?"

"Of course, he's forgiving," spat Stepan.

"Then I suggest you talk to him. I think he already knows your situation, but maybe you better remind him if you think he doesn't."

Stepan walked over to a window and stared out at the village. *What should I do? I feel trapped again. God forgive me.* He turned and walked back to the table, sat down, helped himself to the bread, cheese, and the eggs that were steaming in a bowl. Then slowly he reached for a piece of bacon, hesitated, broke off a piece, and ate it.

"I think my clothes will fit you, Stepan. You're welcome to wear them until we visit the tailor. There are women who will wash your clothes as a service. We're well taken care of. Put these on." Nikolai tossed the clothes to Stepan.

"Thank you," muttered Stepan.

"You're welcome. You change while I finish cleaning up the kitchen. There are many people I want you to meet and things I want to show you. It will help you to get your mind on something else."

When Stepan was ready, they left the house and walked to the main part of the village. Nikolai seemed to be a hero to the entire village and he introduced Stepan to everyone. Many of the younger men hugged Nikolai and shed tears when they saw him. When Nikolai introduced them to Stepan, they hugged him as well. Stepan met so many people that his mind swirled with names.

"I'm not one from this village but they treat me as if I am," marveled Stepan.

"I've trained many of these young men," commented Nikolai. "I've taught them to respect others. They see you as a brother."

"I'm not their brother," spat Stepan. "And quit acting like you're my father.

"I'm not, Stepan. I'm just trying to improve things between us. Will you allow me to do this?"

Stepan shrugged.

"Well, that's a start."

It was dark when they got back to the house. There was no conversation between them.

Stepan walked to his bed. Without changing clothes or washing, he laid down, staring at the ceiling. *I'm exhausted, but I have to have some answers.*

"Nikolai?" he called.

"Yes?"

"How did you become a Cossack?"

"The same way you did."

I'm not surprised. "How old were you?"

"Let's sit. I'll heat up the coffee."

Stepan walked slowly to the kitchen table and sat down. Nikolai poured two cups of coffee and offered Stepan a sweet roll. Stepan shook it off.

Nikolai turned a chair around and straddled it. He took a long drink of the steaming brew. "Twenty years ago. I was twenty-two."

So he's 42. "Do you miss your parents?"

Nikolai didn't answer immediately.

"I'm an orphan. I have no family."

What would it be like to have no family? "You lived alone?"

"No, I lived with different families in the village. The night the Cossack took me, I was with an elderly couple. They were like grandparents to me. He burned their home, but I couldn't get them out. I saved myself and ran. The Cossack shot me in the leg and captured me. I nearly lost my leg from an infection in the wound, but Ludvig nursed me back to health."

"Ludvig?" Stepan sat up.

"Yes. He practiced medicine for many years."

"But . . . he's a cook."

"He is because he saw too many die. He can't bear it anymore. Cooking keeps him out of action."

"Is the Cossack who took you still in the regiment?"

"No. He died shortly after."

"Did you kill him?"

Nikolai paused. "I wanted to—I looked for opportunities,

but I didn't."

"This is why you intimidated me. You thought I was stronger than you? That I might kill you?"

"Ha! Not stronger, but maybe full of more hatred than I."

Several moments passed.

"Stepan, do you know what your name means?"

"Do you mean my real name?"

"No, I mean Stepan."

"No." Stepan admitted.

"It means crown. It's the name of kings, a powerful name—a powerful name for a powerful man."

Stepan didn't know what to say. Thoughts of Momma, Israel, a woman's scream, fires, killing, Papa, kings, and Nikolai swirled through his head. He rose from the table without saying a word and went to bed.

Chapter 15

"Today, you'll start school, Stepan." Nikolai went to the bookcase, pulled a large volume from the shelf, and handed it to Stepan. "This is one of your books."

Stepan looked through some of the pages. "Will you be my teacher?"

"No, it's not allowed."

"Not allowed? Why?"

"I can assist with your learning. I can allow you to practice military tactics with me, but I cannot be your teacher."

"I don't understand."

"You don't have to understand. There are Cossack rules that you must accept without question. You'll understand them in time. However, I'll tell you about this one. Can you deny there's a bond between us?"

Stepan looked away.

"Can you?" Nikolai pressed.

"No."

"If I were your teacher, I might be tempted to show you favor, give you a better grade than you deserve, not push you as hard as the others. Do you understand now?"

"Yes," said Stepan.

"This is better for you. You can ask questions of me you wouldn't be able to ask if I were your teacher. I may not always give you an answer. Some things you'll have to figure out on your own."

Stepan nodded.

"You better eat some breakfast. You'll need nourishment. This is a hard school. Hours of classroom, homework, and practice."

Stepan sat behind a wooden desk. His teacher, Borya Sidorov, was a big man—not fat, but large boned. He stood nearly two hundred centimeters, a giant, and had to duck when he went through doors. His voice commanded attention.

"Vasile," he boomed, "who's the *Okrug Ataman*?"

"Isai Demidov, sir."

"Good. And what does he do, Stepan?"

"He oversees the Don Cossack Okrug."

"Can you be more specific, please?"

"All the Cossacks in the Don River territory are subject to his authority. He distributes the land, makes all military decisions, and reports directly to the tsar."

"Exactly. That's all for today, gentlemen. Tomorrow, we'll discuss the hetman and his council. You may go. Those of you who have a Cossack, report to him."

Stepan gathered his books and headed toward the door.

"Wait, Stepan," called Vasile. "I want to talk to you."

"Fine, let's talk as we walk. Nikolai and I are going fishing."

"Nikolai, Nikolai. Is he the only person in Aksay you socialize with?"

"Why do you ask?"

"Have you noticed the way women look at you?"

"What do you mean?"

"Stepan! Do I have to explain it to you? There isn't a single woman in the village, or probably a married one, who wouldn't jump at the chance of being with you."

Stepan blushed.

"Don't you like girls?" chided Vasile.

"Of course, but I don't have much time for courting."

"Courting? Who said anything about courting? I'm talking about fun. Dancing—and uh . . . well other things." Vasile winked and grinned.

"Oh, I think I understand."

"I'm sure you do. You're a smart man. Why don't you come with me tonight? I have a friend who has a friend who'd like to meet you. She talks about you all the time. All you have to do is say the word and she'd be yours."

"Thanks, Vasile, but no thanks."

"Are you crazy? She's gorgeous. Beautiful brown hair, full lips, long legs . . . "

"I'll see you tomorrow, Vasile. I'm going fishing." Stepan jogged to the house to meet Nikolai.

Summer came to Aksay. Stepan baited his hook, tossed it in the water, and let it sink. He stared at the ripple it created.

"Something on your mind, Stepan?" asked Nikolai.

"Uh no, just tired. The school lessons are intense. They tire my brain." He sat down, crossed his legs, and positioned his pole.

"Ha!" laughed Nikolai. "Borya's a hard teacher—fair but hard. He's the best. You'll learn much from him."

Suddenly Stepan's line went taut, his pole bent, and the fight was on. He yanked the pole back over his left shoulder, jumped to his feet, and pulled the line in steadily—landing a three-pound perch.

"Excellent, Stepan! There's our breakfast. A few more of those and we'll have enough fish for the summer."

They arrived at the house after dark. "Do you have homework?" Nikolai asked.

"Just some reading, I'm ahead of the assignments and I want to stay that way. This way the class is a review and it helps me with the tests."

"Borya tells me you're doing well. He sees you as having leadership qualities."

"What kind of leadership qualities?"

"He didn't say anything in particular. Are you hungry?" Nikolai moved to the cooking area.

Stepan nodded.

"You go ahead and read. I'll put some food together."

Stepan went to the living room, turned up a lamp, and fell into a chair. He tried to read, but found himself staring at the bookcase. He didn't hear Nikolai call him to the table.

"Stepan, are you awake?"

"Uh yes, sorry."

"Come and eat."

Stepan dropped his book on the floor and walked distractedly to the table. Sitting down, he helped himself to some potato dumplings, beans, beets, and bread. There was a cup of coffee steaming beside a piece of pie. He ate slowly without looking up.

"What's troubling you, Stepan? You're not yourself."

"I'm fine, just tired."

"I know what tired looks like. You're distracted. It's like you're thousands of meters away. What's going on? Are you ill?"

"No . . . just . . . well . . . never mind."

"Something's upsetting you. I can see it."

Stepan paused. He put down his bread, took a sip of coffee, and sighed. "Vasile's putting pressure on me."

"Pressure? What kind of pressure."

"He wants me to go dancing with some girl."

"What's wrong with that?"

"Nothing, I guess, if it's only dancing, but it's more than that."

"Oh, I see. He, what can I say, he just wants to use them. And you're not interested?"

"No . . . I mean, I like girls, but I'm not interested in that kind of a relationship."

"Good for you, Stepan. Good for you."

Stepan raised his eyebrows in surprise.

"Oh, you think I'm like Vasile?" asked Nikolai.

"No . . . yes . . . I don't know," said Stepan, squirming in his chair.

"You think because I'm a Cossack, I take women whenever and wherever I want?"

"No, I didn't mean that."

"What did you mean?"

"I don't know, Nikolai. I'm confused. I like girls. I see them looking at me. I'm a man after all, I have feelings and urges. It's just that Momma taught me to treat women with respect. She told me I'd have temptations, but I should wait for the right girl. Getting involved with the wrong one could ruin my happiness for life. I see a girl and I hear Momma."

"I see," said Nikolai. "And this confuses you? I think your Momma is a wise woman who loves you very much. She isn't your problem, Vasile is. He's different from you. He wants you to be like him, but you must be true to yourself, Stepan. You have plenty of time to find the right girl. No need to rush."

Stepan lowered his eyes and then looked at Nikolai.

"Ah, you're wondering how I'd know such a thing."

Stepan put his elbow on the table, laid his forehead in his hand, and shook his head.

"Once I was engaged to be married," confessed Nikolai.

"What happened?"

Nikolai walked over to the stove, poured another cup of coffee for himself, and walked to the window. He took a deep breath and let it out slowly. "I was taken from her."

Stepan lifted his head and leaned forward on both forearms.

"I lived in Włodawa, Poland, on the banks of the Bug

River, just west of the Belarus and Ukrainian borders. Arisha and I were planning to marry. Her family agreed, even though I had no family. Then I was taken. I never saw her again."

"That's terrible. Didn't you try to go back?"

"About five years later, I was on patrol in the area. I inquired about her and found out she and her family had left Poland and gone to America."

"America?"

"A country—actually a continent, thousands of kilometers to the west—across the Atlantic Ocean."

"Why would they go there?"

"It's a land where everyone is free. It's strange, in a way."

"Strange?" asked Stepan curiously.

"Yes. It's a very young country, only a little over a hundred years old, but growing rapidly. Thousands of people from Europe are going there. They say there's much opportunity there, very rich in every way."

"Why didn't you follow her?"

"I thought about it, often, but how would I find her in such a large place? They say there are no boundaries—they can live where they want, travel freely, doing any kind of work they want, not bound to a tsar."

What would that be like? That kind of freedom.

"The *Okhrana*," said Nikolai.

"What?" asked Stepan.

"You asked why I didn't follow her—the *Okhrana* is the reason, the secret police of the tsar. They've existed several years, but were officially established ten years ago after Russian workers attempted to establish trade unions. They fight hostile organizations, terrorists, socialists, and revolutionaries meddling with internal security. The *Okhrana* operates offices throughout the Russian Empire and in major European cities such as Paris and London in an attempt to capture defecting revolutionaries. To fall into their hands would be the worst possible nightmare. It's rumored that they operate torture chambers throughout Russia. They're feared by every Cossack. Down deep, we all want to be free of this life of raiding and pillaging. None of us is here by choice. We'd all find our own freedom tonight if it were possible. You're surprised to hear me talk this way?"

"Yes," confessed Stepan. "You told me we are freemen."

Nikolai ignored the comment. "There isn't a night goes by that I don't think of Arisha —wondering where she is, what she's doing. What our life would have been like together. Children."

"Is there no other in your life?"

"There's one here I'm fond of—Tatyana. She'd marry me if I asked, but I can't let go of Arisha. She stole my heart and won't let go."

Silence filled the house like a heavy fog.

"Someday you'll meet such a woman, Stepan. To throw yourself away for anyone less would be a waste for you. Let Vasile do what he wants with his life. You . . . you take the higher road."

Stepan nodded, took another sip of coffee, and finished

his meal. He cleared the table and washed the dishes.

"Do you want to say anything else, Stepan?"

"No, thank you."

"I'll see you in the morning then. Sleep well."

Stephen went back to the living room chair, sat down, and stared through the window to a place thousands of kilometers west. *America—a free country. Live anywhere you want. Wouldn't that be something?*

Chapter 16

The summer and fall flew by. Stephan was gathering his books at the end of the school day. He didn't see Nikolai enter the classroom. "Happy birthday, Stepan," shouted Nikolai.

"Happy birthday," echoed Stepan's classmates and friends.

Nikolai placed a cake on Stephan's desk. Vasile stood on a desk and raised his hand in a mock salute. "Salute to the newest seventeen-year-old in the settlement."

"Salute," repeated the others imitating Vasile's gesture.

The Commander entered the room. "May I have your attention, gentlemen."

A hush came over the group. Everyone turned toward the Commander.

"I hate to disturb your birthday celebration, Stepan. It was my intent to celebrate with you, but there's been a meeting called by the *Okrug Ataman*. This isn't just a council meeting—everyone is required to attend. The meeting will be in the combat training area. Be there in fifteen minutes. Cossacks will meet with me at the stables immediately. "

Stepan looked at Nikolai. Nikolai shrugged his shoulders, raised his eyebrows, and then nodded toward the meeting place.

Stepan and his friends burst into conversation as they

walked toward the gathering. "What do you think it's about?" asked Stepan.

Aleks spoke, "I expect this has to do with events Mr. Sidorov has been telling us about. He said he fears this time to be the worst year in Russian history."

"1905? Why?" asked Dmitri. "Russia has been involved in conflict constantly in her history."

"Not an internal revolution like this one, according to Mr. Sidorov," said Misha. "Weren't you there when he talked to us after school the other day? He said much of the Russian population is angry with the tsar for what happened on Bloody Sunday."

"No, it must have been the day I had to take care of the horses," replied Dmitri. "What did he say?"

"I remember!" exclaimed Mikhail. "He said there were two hundred thousand workers organized to strike by a priest. The priest led them in a march on the winter palace of the tsar. Can you believe it? The Imperial Army stopped them. Mr. Sidorov said there were nearly a thousand killed or wounded—even women and children."

"It was bad," said Aleks, "and now it's led to a revolution of strikers all over the country."

"Not only that," said Volya, "Mr. Sidorov said the war with Japan has been extremely costly—110,000 troops lost and sixty ships captured or destroyed. He said he doesn't see how things can get any worse."

Stepan found himself being pushed into the crowd of hundreds of Cossacks just as the Commander appeared. As the Commander raised his hands to quiet the throng, seven men wearing Russian Army uniforms walked in and stood behind him.

One of them whispered something to the Commander.

"Gentlemen . . . ," the Commander hesitated, looked toward the ceiling as if searching for words, and then cleared his throat.

"Get out of the way," said the man who had whispered to the Commander and roughly pushed him aside.

A whisper ran through the crowd.

"You are now part of the Russian Army. You are no longer Cossacks, not the freemen you have been."

There was an outburst among the men. "Quiet!" demanded the speaker.

The eruption continued. A rifle shot silenced the crowd.

"Your Commander will give you more information. Your settlement is surrounded by Russian soldiers. Do not try to rebel or escape. They have orders to shoot to kill." He turned and pushed his way through the six soldiers. They followed him into the darkness.

"What is he talking about?" yelled a Cossack. Several others demanded to know.

The Commander raised his hands. Several minutes went by before he attempted to speak over the noise of the Cossacks.

"I know you're wondering what has happened, how this could happen. I'll tell you so you'll know the truth and won't be confused by rumors. Russia has been at war with Japan and has lost hundreds of thousands of soldiers."

"What does this have to do with us?" shouted someone behind Stepan.

The men responded with a rumble of comments. Again, the Commander raised his hands to quiet the crowd.

"We have been drafted into the Russian Army. Our land is at stake . . . our homes. Our hetman, *Okrug Ataman*, myself, and your Cossacks are Russian officers. There is an incident in Odessa that requires our involvement. Half of you men will be leaving in the morning for Odessa, the remainder will stay here as a reserve. Find your Cossack to receive further instructions. That is all." The Commander left the area.

The men stood stunned, then gradually dispersed. Stepan looked for Nikolai and saw him standing under a tree. Stepan ran to him.

"What is happening? What is the Commander talking about? Are we really Russian soldiers now?"

Nikolai nodded.

"Jews are leading a rebellion against the tsar—the revolution has swept over all Russia. We are going to Odessa to stop them there."

Stepan's heart almost stopped. "We're going to kill Jews?"

Nikolai placed his hand on Stepan's shoulder. Stepan jerked away. Nikolai took him by the arm. "Listen to me, Stepan!"

"No! I'm a Jew!" cried Stepan.

Nikolai looked around nervously. "Stepan! Control yourself!"

"It's a pogrom isn't it? We're going to kill Jews. Would they kill me? My friends—would they kill me, Nikolai?" Stepan began to pace back and forth, kicking dirt and rocks.

"Stepan, don't make this an issue between us."

Stepan stopped. He narrowed his eyes at Nikolai. "What do you mean, don't make this an issue between us?"

"I'm your Cossack. Do you understand what I'm saying? I'm responsible for you—and for what you say and do."

The reality of what Nikolai was saying came crashing down on Stepan like a boulder. *He'll forcibly take me to the Commander. . . to Odessa.* He put his hands over his face and shook his head.

Nikolai put his arm around Stepan's shoulders and walked him to the house.

The next morning, they were back at the meeting place. The area was ringed with Russian soldiers. The Commander's voice cut through the air. "Gentlemen, I know all of you are anxious to go to Odessa, but as I told you last night, half of you will stay here in Aksay."

"Why?" shouted Kirill.

The Cossacks grumbled.

"Men," called the Commander raising his voice, "Those of you who are not going will be a reserve contingency. Behind me is a table. Walk by the table in a single file. Each of you will be given a piece of paper. Those of you who have a black dot will be going to Odessa. The rest of you will remain here. Those of you who are going, prepare yourself and report back here in one hour."

Stepan got in line. He hesitantly took the paper handed to him, crumpled it, and put it in his pocket. In the house, he went to his room and sat on the bed. *God, don't let me go.* He pulled the wadded piece of paper from his pocket. With eyes closed, he smoothed it. Slowly he opened his eyes. It was blank. He turned it over and stared at the blank paper. *Thank you, God.* Stepan closed his eyes and breathed in deeply, letting his breath out slowly.

As the weeks went by, news of the conflict in Odessa filtered back to Aksay. Stepan and Nikolai learned that eight hundred Jews had been killed and several thousand wounded. Stepan was devastated. "This is horrible, Nikolai. How can I be a Cossack when we're doing this to my people?"

"We're not doing anything to anyone," replied Nikolai. "We're here in Aksay, not in Odessa. I'm not trying to be mean. I know it's a very bad situation for everyone. I know it's extremely difficult for you, but you can't let your fear of going to Odessa control you. You must keep your wits about you, maintain your studies, and live your life."

"Live my life? When I know that at any moment I can be placed in that horrible situation? It's your fault that I'm here. You kidnapped me. You took my life away from me."

"I did what I had to do. It was war that night, just like this is war. We were Russians, freemen, Cossacks under the order of the hetman—ultimately the tsar."

"Freemen? Ha!" spat Stepan. He threw his hat on the

ground. "This isn't war. This is a slaughter of defenseless people."

"Be careful what you say and do, Stepan. You can say anything to me, but guard your words around others. Don't forget what you are—a Russian soldier. Don't make it dangerous for yourself—or me. To display hostility could cost you your life . . . and mine."

Stepan nodded. He picked up his hat and brushed it off angrily.

The days went by in slow motion.

This is agony. I could be called to go to Odessa today. It's hard to do what the Commander demands of me—preparing myself to kill Jews. Nikolai was right, it's good that he's not my teacher. At least I can talk to him about my anger.

One evening, Stepan sat with his friends after three hours of sword drill. He rubbed his right shoulder. "I don't think I can lift my arm again."

The others laughed knowingly.

Vasile sat down beside Stepan. "I've never worked so hard," said Vasile. "Have you?"

"No. I thought I'd get used to it, but every day seems harder. My muscles are growing, but my sword seems to get heavier."

"You're doing well, though, Stepan. I'm not sure I could take you. You've beaten almost everyone who's challenged you."

"We're bound to be pitted against each other soon."

"No, we won't. I'm going to Odessa," said Vasile.

Stepan turned toward him. "How do you know?"

"Aleksandr just told me. There will be a new company. Aleksandr has been promoted to commander and will lead us. I'm sure that's why I'm going."

"Am I going?' asked Stepan, dreading the answer.

"No."

Thank you, God. Thank you.

"How do you feel about it, Vasile?" Stepan asked hesitantly.

"I'm ready to go."

Stepan nodded. "When do you leave?"

"At first light."

"Does Anna know?"

"Not yet. I'm going to her house now. It's going to be hard for her. I think she wants to marry me," Vasile smiled.

"Do you love her?"

"I don't know. I do know I don't want to marry her. Not now. Who would want to get married in this madness?

Stepan nodded his head. "I'll be there in the morning—to tell you good-bye."

The two friends hugged each other.

"God be with you, Vasile."

"Thank you, Stepan."

Vasile turned toward Anna's house and Stepan toward Nikolai's.

Chapter 17

During the next several months, the soldiers remaining at home perfected their military tactics. They spent long days in class receiving instruction and weeks on patrol practicing what they learned.

On one such patrol, Stepan and Nikolai had been away nearly two months. It was nearing evening, almost time to set up camp for the night. Stepan and Nikolai patrolled together, Aza lazily walking in front of Nikolai's horse. Stepan held Aza's reins loosely with his left hand, his right leg hooked around the saddle horn. He was reading a Russian history book, lying in his lap.

Nikolai pulled up beside him. "You're going to be more educated than I," laughed Nikolai.

"You may be right," kidded Stepan. Then he turned serious. "I'd like to be a person of means someday."

"I think you can be whatever you want to be, Stepan. You're a gifted man. You learn quickly."

Stepan leaned back in his saddle, his hands behind his head, fingers intertwined. He sighed deeply.

"What are you thinking about?" asked Nikolai.

"Momma and Israel."

"I've been thinking about them, too." Nikolai hesitated as if he was searching for something.

"Thinking about Momma and Israel?" asked Stepan surprised.

"Why don't you go seen them?"

Stepan sat up with a start, mouth open, eyes wide. His book fell to the ground. He grabbed Aza's reins and pulled back hard.

"Do you mean it, Nikolai?"

Nikolai held his own horse steady, calming him. "Yes," he said with a laugh. "It can be arranged. I've suggested it to the Commander."

"And he's agreed?"

"But of course. I requested it," laughed Nikolai.

"I don't know what to say."

"There's nothing to say, Stepan. You're a man, a trusted man. There isn't a soldier in the regiment who wouldn't want you backing him up in battle or who wouldn't give you anything you might need. Besides, you're a freeman." Nikolai smiled.

"We both know that's not true, Nikolai. We've been through this before—more than once. We're almost serfs. We were purchased with this land. I mean, we own the land, but we gave up our freedom when we accepted it. We're not attached to the land like serfs, but we're under the control of the tsar. Isn't it true?"

Nikolai nodded his head slowly. "It's hard to admit the truth. Sometimes I think we're little boys dressed in costumes."

"You know that isn't true either. We're still Cossacks—

Russian Cossacks. We're freemen in everything else, but we must go where the tsar tells us to go and do what he tells us to do. Odessa's proof of that to me."

"You're right, Stepan. You see it as is. I see it as I wish it to be."

Stepan climbed off Aza and retrieved his book. He tucked it into a saddlebag. Climbing back on his horse, he asked, "When can I leave?"

"As soon as we get home—we'll be out another two weeks. I've some more news for you; Vasile will be home in two weeks."

"Wonderful! Do you think he can go with me? We've talked of this so often."

"That is up to Aleksandr."

"Do you think he'll allow Vasile to go?"

"That's a good question. Aleksandr's a hard man. All Vasile can do is ask." Nikolai paused. "Do you think Vasile would come back? I've no doubt about you, but Vasile . . . I wonder."

"I believe he would. He has nothing in Gagra to keep him. I think he's just curious about the village and would get excited about the possibility of taking the trip. I know he'd like to visit his parents' graves." Stepan thought for a moment. "If Vasile should not come back, would I be held accountable to Aleksandr, the Commander, or worse, the *Okrug Ataman*?"

"Why would you be? Vasile doesn't answer to you. In fact, he's older by two years. Besides, you're like brothers."

"Yes, we are, but it's always been hard to know what he's

thinking. I think he carries a lot of feelings within."

"Nevertheless, it's your choice whether to invite him or not. You're not obligated to take him with you, nor are you obligated to see that he returns with you."

"I'll ask him and leave it up to him."

Stepan was quiet. *Momma. Israel. What will it be like to see them again?*

Stepan broke the silence, "Vasile will probably only have two weeks. Riding over the mountains would take too long."

"If Aleksandr lets him go, I suspect he would give him more time considering," said Nikolai. "Or there's another way. You can take a boat to Pitsunda."

"We can't take our horses on the boat."

"No, but it's less than twenty kilometers from Pitsunda to Gagra. That'd be a good walk for you, or if you're lazy, you can rent horses or get a ride on a cart."

"Lazy! I run circles around you."

"Ha!" laughed Nikolai. He kicked his horse in the flanks and took off at a gallop.

Aza jumped. Stepan pulled the reins tight and tried to stay in his saddle. "I'll get you for this," he yelled. Taking Aza to a gallop, Stepan chased Nikolai into the camp.

After they brushed down and fed their horses, the two men walked toward the food wagon.

"Coffee, Nikolai?" asked Stepan.

"Sure, black. I'll get us a plate of food," said Nikolai. "Meet under the tree?"

Stepan nodded.

When they reached the tree, Stepan handed a steaming cup to Nikolai. "This'll make you feel better."

"Feel better about what?"

"About having less brains than I," said Stepan laughing.

"Don't let it go to your head. It was a weak moment for me."

They finished their goulash and were sipping their coffee when Stepan broke the silence. "Nikolai?"

"Yes."

"Thank you. My life is more than I hoped for."

Two weeks later, they arrived in Aksay well after dark.

"I'll take care of the horses," said Stepan.

"I'll fix us some supper," said Nikolai as he headed toward the house.

Stepan entered the house to the smell of bacon. "Breakfast?"

"It's easy and fast. And I'm hungry. Aren't you?"

"Very. The last day always seems to be the longest. I've been thinking all day of how good my bed's going to feel."

"I'm glad tomorrow's Saturday. We can sleep late and relax all day."

"That sounds wonderful," replied Stepan.

Stepan awoke to a pounding on the front door. The sun was shining through his bedroom window telling him it was well into the morning. Grabbing his robe, he went to the door.

"Vasile!"

"How are you, my friend?"

"Good. Come in." Vasile stepped through the door and the two friends hugged. "Nikolai told me you were coming. How long do you have?"

"Two weeks. I'll probably sleep half of it," laughed Vasile.

"You do look tired, older," observed Stepan.

"Speaking of older, you're eighteen now."

"Yes. It's hard to believe a year has passed in some ways. No party this year, just Nikolai, Ludvig, me at the house. Coffee?"

"Yes, thanks. How's school?"

"School is good. I'm learning history, math, and science. Nikolai's teaching me to speak Low German."

"Are you learning military strategy?"

"Of course, I learn tactics in the classroom, practice with Nikolai, and go on patrol."

"Do you have any girlfriends?"

"Several," laughed Stepan.

Vasile looked at him out of the corner of his eye, "Really?"

"Really. I've lots of *girl friends*."

"I see. You should see the women in Odessa. They like soldiers. If you're ever transferred there, I'll introduce you to several. You can take your pick."

"Thank you," replied Stepan.

"Well, that's a change," Vasile acknowledged.

"What?"

"You thanked me."

"Well, I do have manners," Stepan smiled.

Vasile laughed. "Yes, you do. Yes, you do."

"What about Anna? She's really missed you. It nearly killed her when you left."

"Anna? I'll see her, but . . . well, she's just a friend. We've exchanged letters. I told her how I feel about marriage."

"Only a friend? I thought you loved her."

"Like I said, there are several ladies in Odessa." Vasile winked.

Stepan shook his head. Vasile laughed.

"I have a question to ask you, Vasile. Would you like to go to Gagra with me?"

"Gagra? Are you serious?"

"Yes." Stepan told Vasile about the conversation with Nikolai.

"When can we leave?"

Stepan smiled. "Probably tomorrow, if Aleksandr agrees."

"If Aleksandr agrees? Do you think I need his permission?"

"Of course . . . he's your . . ." Stepan said surprised.

"Cossack?" Vasile laughed. "He's in Odessa. I'm here and I have two weeks. How long are you planning to be gone?"

Stepan shook his head. "If we go by boat to Pitsunda and back, it'll take two days each way, another two days for travel to and from Gagra, and two days for visiting."

"That's eight days. I have plenty of time. Tomorrow it is."

Chapter 18

The sun reflected off the Black Sea. Stepan and Vasile leaned across the boat's rail looking toward Gagra and the Caucasus Mountains. Stepan scanned the scenery, remembering childhood activities.

"I remember the first time I fished in these waters—how much I struggled with throwing my line and bait out far enough. Papa showed me repeatedly how to do it. I thought the first big fish I caught was going to pull me in. Papa told me repeatedly, 'Pull, you can do it.' I was so proud when I landed it. He picked me up and swung me around with his head tilted back, laughing and shouting, 'That's my boy, that's my boy! I knew you could do it.' Then he showed me how to clean the fish. When we got home, Momma made it a bigger event by fixing my favorite foods, potato dumplings and fish pie."

"I remember your papa. He was a big man and he always laughed."

"I remember yours too." Stepan stopped short when the memory of a scream roared into his mind.

"What's wrong?" Vasile asked.

"I'm just nervous. I haven't seen Momma for two years. Maybe she won't like the way I am now."

"Of course she will. You haven't changed that much."

"Maybe not physically, but in my mind and my thinking, I'm not the same person. Are you?"

"Does it matter? There's no one there for me."

"Of course there is, Vasile. Momma always treated you like a son. Israel is your brother, too. The whole village is your family."

"Thanks, Stepan. I'm here to support you, though. Neither of us have a home there anymore. We live in a different world now."

"I'm sorry, Vasile. I'm being extremely selfish. I haven't been considering you. Please forgive me."

"You're forgiven."

"No. I mean . . . you're right. I've been thinking only of myself. Not just today, but all along. We've never talked about that night in regard to your . . . your loss. Did you ever talk to anyone about it?"

"No. Well, once I started to, but we got interrupted. I don't have anyone like Nikolai in my life. You're lucky, Stepan."

Stepan was surprised by the remark. *I'm fortunate. I never thought of Vasile's perspective of my relationship with Nikolai.*

"Do you want to talk about it now, Vasile?"

Vasile paused. "I . . . ." The air was thick between them. "I miss them so much. They never had a chance. If only Father had stayed in the house. He . . . he would still be alive . . . and so would Mother. I tried to stop him, but he ran out of the house with his rifle. He didn't get ten steps before he was shot."

Vasile's voice became hard and cold. "Mother ran out of the house to him. She was bending over him when a Cossack ran toward her. She had Father's pistol. She stood up screaming, pointed the pistol at him, but it didn't fire. I don't think it was loaded. The Cossack thrust her through with his sword—her scream was cut short. I didn't do anything. I hear her scream nearly every night."

"What could you have possibly done?" Stepan tried to comfort his friend.

"I don't know. I've asked myself that question a thousand times. I had no weapon, I was stunned, I stumbled out of the house to my parents. That's when I was captured. I watched a Cossack set fire to our house. It was horrible."

Stepan had no words for his friend. Even if he did, he wouldn't have been able to speak them. They would have only choked in his throat and started an avalanche of tears.

The two friends slipped into silence. The sounds of the boat, the water, and the wind lulled them into meditation.

Stepan slumped. A heavy sadness fell over him. *I won't believe I'm home until I'm looking at Momma and Israel—touching and holding them.*

They had been walking nearly three hours. The moon had barely crested the mountains; the houses came into view as they topped a hill on the south side of Gagra. Stepan caught his breath. There stood his house. It was exactly the way he remembered it . . . the barn off to the left . . . his eyes were drawn to the cellar. The sights, sounds, and smells of that night flashed through his mind. The memory of Nikolai penetrated the vision. Stepan felt overwhelmed.

"You all right?" asked Vasile huskily.

Stepan cleared his throat. "I think so. I need a few minutes."

The two men stood in silence as they surveyed the village. No one was in sight.

"They're all eating supper, I think," said Stepan.

"Maybe your momma has enough for us."

"She always cooked more than enough. I'm drooling just thinking about what's on that table."

Stepan started down the hill toward his house. Vasile followed. Just as they neared the house, the backdoor opened. A figure stepped out.

"It's Israel," whispered Stepan. "He's much taller! He's going to the barn; I'm going after him."

Thoughts of that night raced through his head. *Don't scare him any more than you have to. What are you thinking, Stepan? You're not wearing a Cossack's uniform.*

He walked up to the barn door and pushed it open. "It's me, Israel. Nathan."

"Nathan?" Israel asked unbelieving.

"Yes, Israel. It's me." Stepan stepped forward throwing both arms around Israel. Tears flowed down his cheeks as he pulled Israel tight.

Israel sobbed. "N . . . Nathan, I thought I'd never see you again!" he stammered.

"Yes. Vasile is with me."

"Vasile!"

"Hello, Israel," said Vasile. "You've grown."

"How's Momma?" Stepan asked.

"Oh, Momma," gasped Israel. "She's going to faint when she sees you!"

"Is she all right?"

"Yes. She talks about you every day. She's never given up hope of seeing you again. We pray for you all the time . . . and Vasile."

"I'd like to see Momma alone first," said Stepan huskily.

In less than a minute, he was at the back door. He took a deep breath and pushed the door open.

"Israel, get in here. Your supper is getting cold."

"It's me, Nathan, Momma."

Momma froze. A ladle fell to the floor. "Nathan?" she said weakly.

"Yes, Momma. Stepan stepped into the room."

Turning slowly she cried, "Nathan? . . . Nathan!" She ran to him and fell into his open arms.

Stepan felt her warm kisses and tears all over his face. "Momma, I've missed you so much! I love you."

Momma stepped back, holding Nathan's face in the palms of her hands. "Oh, Nathan, I love you so much, my son. I knew you'd come back to me. I knew you were alive. Where have you been?" She searched his eyes. "Thank you, God. Nathan, I'm so glad you're home. Now we're a family again."

Stepan stiffened. "For two days, Momma."

Disappointment clouded her face and just as quickly

disappeared, replaced by a smile. "You're here, Nathan. You're here. I must get Israel."

"He's waiting outside, Momma. He knows I'm here."

"You always were a romantic, Nathan, always wanting to surprise me." Stepan pulled away from Momma and opened the back door. Vasile and Israel stepped in.

Looking over Stepan's shoulder, she said "Vasile." She stepped forward, reached out, and touched Vasile's face with the tips of her fingers. "Dear Vasile, I've thought of you so often and wondered if you were alive with Nathan."

Vasile was unable to speak.

"You must be starved," said Momma.

"Let's eat," said Israel. "You remember Momma's cooking, don't you, Nathan?"

"Remember it! I've dreamed about it. Vasile and I talked about it all the way here. I know that smell, Momma. No one makes venison stew like you do, or gooseberry cobbler."

After supper, Stepan insisted Momma sit while he, Vasile, and Israel cleaned the table and did the dishes. Then they joined her at the table.

"Thank you, gentlemen," said Momma. Then she looked at Vasile. "Vasile, I don't know how to say this . . . I know you must wonder about your parents."

The room became silent. Vasile spoke softly, "I know they both died. They were dead before I was taken."

"I'm relieved you know. I've been afraid you didn't know and you would always wonder about them. We buried them north of the village where the stream turns south. I visit them often and keep their graves respectful. The whole village takes care of them."

"I'm grateful . . . ." Vasile choked on his words and nodded.

Momma got up, walked to Vasile, and placed her hands on each side of his face. "I know I can never replace your mother, Vasile, but I consider you to be one of my sons. I will be your Momma from now on, if you want me to. You can call me Momma. You're part of our family. We all love you."

No one spoke for several minutes. The sound of the fire crackling in the stove covered the silence.

"Thank you, Momma," said Vasile.

"I'm one of the hunters now," beamed Israel.

"I don't doubt it. You've become a man. Who taught you?" asked Stepan.

"The men in the village taught me how to shoot. They took care of me. They helped Momma with the chores, even the dishes, if you can believe it, so I could spend time in the woods."

"They never did that for me," laughed Stepan. "But you were the dishwasher then." He winked at Israel. "I'm very proud of you, Israel. You've really become a man. Papa would be proud of you, too."

"Nathan, what happened? Where did you go, what happened to you?" asked Momma.

"I'm a soldier, Momma."

Tears came to her eyes.

"It's all right Momma," said Stepan.

"How can it be all right, Nathan? You're a child. My baby, how can it be all right?" she cried.

Stepan placed his hand on hers. "It's all right, Momma. I'm well. I'm a man. Healthy. Respected. It's not the life you wanted for me, but it's a good life. I'm in school." Stepan was surprised to hear the words that came from his mouth. Yet, he knew they were true. He said with deep sincerity, "It cannot be changed, Momma."

Momma stared at him with sad eyes, but then the corners of her mouth curled into a slight smile. She nodded. "I understand, my son. Let's enjoy our time together."

Has she accepted the situation?

The two days went fast. Stepan and Vasile reacquainted themselves with the village, but Stepan spent as much time with Momma and Israel as he could. *In a way, it's like I've never left.* Israel showed Stepan his marksmanship.

"You're very good, Israel. I'm proud of you and I'm sure Momma is too."

"I think she is," said Israel. "I'm glad you've come back, Nathan. It'll be much better for Momma knowing you are alive. Often, she would stare out the window. I know she was thinking about you and hoping you'd come walking up to the house."

"I knew she was thinking about me—you as well, Israel."

"It's been hard on both of us. What's it like, Nathan?"

"Be grateful you're here with Momma. Take care of her."

Israel nodded. There was no more talk of the matter

between them.

"It's very hard to see you go again, Nathan," said Momma as she gathered him in her arms.

"I know, Momma. It's hard for me too, but at least this time, you know I'm well."

"I'll always worry about you, Nathan. I'll never stop thinking of you. My love is with you every moment of every day."

"I feel it, Momma. My love is with you too." He kissed her on the cheek and pulled away from her embrace. Tears streaked her face. He wiped them away and stepped out the door. Vasile and Israel were waiting outside. The three walked up the hill together. At the top, Stepan hugged Israel and kissed him on his forehead. Stepan turned toward the house, waved to Momma, and put his hand on Vasile's shoulder. The two turned away and disappeared over the hill.

On the road back to Pitsunda, Vasile broke the silence. "I went to visit their graves. I wanted to tell them good-bye."

After a few meters, Stepan asked, "How are you, my friend?"

"I feel a strange peace. I told them I'm all right and that I love them. Then I told them good-bye."

"Are you angry?" asked Stepan.

"I've been angry since that night. I have always felt there was something I could've done to protect them."

"Do you really think so?"

"Not now. I wanted to get even, somehow, for a long time. It's strange . . . now the regiment is my family. They're my friends. I don't even know who killed my family. It was too quick—too confusing. I've wondered if their killer is still alive. No one has said anything to me."

Silence.

"What about you? Are you angry about what's happened to you? Don't you want to get even?" asked Vasile.

"I did for a long time. I hated Nikolai. I used to wake up in the night and watch him sleeping. I would think I could kill him in his sleep, but I knew I couldn't. Even if I could, I'd never get out of camp alive. Now, I fear his dying. It's really very hard to understand. I'm different now. I'm a soldier and this is my life. I don't know when I'll ever see Momma and Israel again, but bad memories have been replaced by good. Momma knows I'm well. I know she and Israel are healthy and Israel is taking care of her. He's replaced me as the man of the house. They're in no danger. Life is strange," said Stepan. "Very strange."

Chapter 19

"How was your visit, Stepan?" Nikolai asked.

"It was wonderful seeing Momma and Israel. Momma looked tired at first, but she looked better when I left. Knowing I'm all right gave her peace of mind. Israel is becoming a man."

"I'm glad to hear they're well . . . and how was it for Vasile?"

Stepan rubbed his brow then smoothed back his hair. "He saw his parents' grave. I think it was good for him to be there. It's behind him now. He left for Odessa this morning. He said there's nothing for him here," said Stepan.

"What about his girlfriend?" asked Nikolai.

"That's over. He has a girlfriend in Odessa."

"Is he serious about her?"

"Ha! No, I think it's a game to him. As long as he has a girlfriend where he is, that's all he cares about."

"I see," said Nikolai. "I suppose being a soldier serves him well in that area."

"I suppose. He doesn't seem like he's twenty years old. He's more like a little boy playing games."

Nikolai nodded. "There are many like him. Conflict seems to be their life. As for you, young man, are you ready to get back to school?

"Strangely, I missed it. My friends are here and I'm looking forward to seeing them. I better do some reading. My classmates have probably caught up with me. I don't want to give them any false hope of passing me."

Nikolai laughed. He put his arm around Stepan and hugged him. "I'll leave you alone. I'm going to visit Tatyana. She is fixing my favorite meal tonight. Do you want me to bring some back for you?"

"Tatyana, hmm?" teased Stepan. "Sure, she's a good cook. Tell her hello for me."

"I'll see you in the morning," Nikolai left with a grin. "Don't wait up for me."

"I won't."

Stepan celebrated his twentieth birthday in Aksay. He finished school at the top of his class.

"I'm very proud of you, Stepan," said Nikolai. "How does it feel to be done with school?"

"Good in some ways. I'll miss it. I can't help but wonder what comes next."

"I can tell you, if you really want to know," said Nikolai, his voice turning serious.

Stepan's look was curious. "What kind of a statement is that?"

"A sober one. You're going to Odessa."

Stepan's heart stopped. "Odessa! Why? Things are much quieter there. They haven't sent soldiers in months."

"The *Okrug Ataman* has ordered it. That's all you need to

know."

'What am I going to do, Nikolai? This is impossible." In desperation, Stepan slammed his hands against his forehead. Through gritted teeth he whispered, "I can't kill Jews! I can't! Could you kill Russians?"

"I'm a soldier. I do what I must do," Nikolai countered.

"I can't. I won't."

"Will you desert and bring the *Okhrana* down on yourself? Will you make an enemy of me? You're a soldier. You'll do what you must do."

Clenching his fists in anger, Stephen whirled and ran toward the woods.

The following morning, at dawn, thirty soldiers met in the center of the city. As the sun rose, the soldiers left Aksay through a cheering crowd. Their saddlebags were loaded with sweets, black bread, and small gifts. Except for Stepan, there was excited conversation among them. Nikolai tried to engage him in small talk, but Stepan ignored his attempts. Occasionally, Stepan drew a curious look from some of his friends, but their excitement kept them engaged in constant chatter.

After an hour, Stepan finally broke his silence. "How long will it take to get there?" he asked.

Nikolai looked at him and smiled. "A month . . . maybe longer."

They made camp that night along a stream.

"I miss Ludvig's coffee," said Stepan. "This is good, but

it's not Ludvig's."

"I think Ludvig has made his last pot of coffee on the trail. He's ready to stay home and let a younger one take his place."

"Who could do that?" asked Stepan.

"He's trained two or three. He's been generous with his recipes."

"Is one of them with us?"

"No," laughed Nikolai. "We're on our own this time. We have to put up with a month of our own cooking."

Stepan groaned.

They arrived in Odessa as the sun was setting. A golden glow lit the water of the port. There was a beauty in spite of the obvious destruction.

"Odessa's different than I expected," said Stepan, looking around.

"The weather's much milder here," replied Nikolai. "It's an important Russian port and has become the fourth largest city in Imperial Russia. You can see the architectural style is more Mediterranean than Russian."

They spotted a soldier, no one they knew, and asked directions to the headquarters. As soon as they reported in, they were directed to the stables and the barracks. Stepan took his saddle off Aza and rubbed him down. He poured some oats in a feeder. "Here's your new home, Aza."

Stepan and Nikolai walked to the barracks. Stepan looked around with disapproval. Several men lounged around—reading, talking, playing chess, writing letters, or sleeping.

"It's dingy and dirty," Stepan observed.

"Yes, but it's dry," said Nikolai. "And we have bunks to sleep on. It'll be better than sleeping on the ground."

Stepan shrugged. He spotted two empty bunks together and asked an older soldier standing close by, "Are these bunks taken?"

"No, they're yours if you want them. Any bunk that doesn't have a towel hanging on the end is available."

"Thank you," said Stepan, looking around for Nikolai. He saw him walking toward the back of the barracks.

Stepan hurried to him. "Nikolai, I've found two bunks for us over there." Stepan pointed to a window.

"No, Stepan, I have to sleep back there." He pointed to a door at the back of the barracks. "Now that we're a part of the Russian army, we're on different levels. I'm now an officer, and I have to sleep with others who are of the same rank."

"You mean I have to salute you?"

"Yes," said Nikolai, laughing. "I am an officer. I'll be back as soon as I put my stuff away."

Stepan watched Nikolai go through the door then turned back to the bunk he selected. It was a lower one. He tossed his hat on it, put his belongings in a trunk at the foot of the bed, hung his coat on a rack, and tested the mattress. It was firm, but comfortable. *I can sleep on this. It's not like the bed at Nikolai's, but it's softer than sleeping on the ground and it's warm.*

"How does it feel, Stepan?" asked Nikolai.

Stepan jumped. "I must have dozed off. I didn't hear you."

"You haven't been in the Imperial Army for one day and you're already getting careless."

"No, I'm not. I'm going to look for Vasile."

"I'm going to find the dining hall," replied Nikolai. "Meet you there."

Stepan filled his plate with hot food. He saw Nikolai and some of the others eating. Stepan joined them.

"Did you find Vasile?" asked Nikolai.

"I found out about him. He's in the same barracks with us, but he has a job in the pharmacy.

"The pharmacy? That's rich duty," replied Nikolai in mild surprise. "He must know somebody. That's usually reserved for special soldiers."

"What do you mean?" asked Stepan.

"Usually an army officer or the son of some important official gets that kind of duty."

Stepan raised an eyebrow.

Nikolai shrugged.

They finished their meal and returned to the barracks. As they stepped through the door, Vasile's voice boomed as he walked toward them.

"Welcome to Odessa, Stepan. Hello, Nikolai."

The three hugged and shook hands.

"I'm told you've found your bunks. Mine is here by the door. I'm in charge of the barracks. If you have any questions or problems come see me. If you cause any problems, I'll come see you," he said with a wink. "You'll find that, although it's a bit plain, it's comfortable. Are you hungry?"

"We've just finished eating," said Stepan.

"Did you enjoy the food? It isn't as good as Ludvig's; nevertheless, it's pleasant."

"It was good," said Nikolai.

"Let me show you around the post," said Vasile. "It's been an interesting time here. There has been much killing. There was even a mutiny by the sailors on a Russian warship who turned their guns on the Imperial headquarters."

"Russians fighting Russians?" asked Stepan.

"It was a short-lived altercation. The ship sailed to Romania—right through a Russian blockade safely because Russian sailors refused to fire on it. Romania refused to give them supplies and the mutineers eventually turned the ship over to Romanian authorities. I don't know what happened after that. Nothing good, I'm sure."

"What will you and I be doing here, Nikolai?" asked Stepan.

"We're part of a reserve contingency for security. If there are any outbreaks against the Imperial Army, we'll be called in to police the area."

"Police? But we're soldiers!"

"Things are changing," said Nikolai looking down at the floor.

"What's the threat now?" asked Stepan.

Nikolai turned to Vasile.

"The tsar has imposed a draft to replace lost troops," said Vasile. "This isn't popular with the people and there's a great resistance. Anger's rising. This is why you're here."

"So it'll be up to us to patrol the streets and curb any demonstrations?" asked Stepan.

"Yes. Soldiers are being pulled in from all over Russia to show a presence of force to put down the resistance," replied Vasile.

"Are the Jews demonstrating?" whispered Stepan.

"It's the unions. There may be Jews involved," said Vasile.

"We better clean our guns," said Nikolai. "It sounds like we'll be seeing action."

"You might be interested in this, Nikolai." Vasile pulled out a revolver. "The Imperial Army has more modern weapons—multiple-firing revolvers, rifles, and fast firing weapons called machine guns. This is a Nagant M1895 revolver. It holds seven bullets that can be fired without reloading."

Nikolai reached for the weapon. Vasile handed it to him saying, "Be careful, Nikolai. It's loaded. If you pull back the hammer, it can be fired with a slight pull of the trigger."

"Do the union men have these?" asked Nikolai, handing the gun to Stepan.

"No, unless they've taken them from soldiers who've died in the fighting," replied Vasile.

"It's heavier than my pistol," said Stepan.

Vasile nodded. He pulled out a bullet and handed it to Nikolai. "This is what it fires. Everything—flint, cap, and powder—is inside. After firing, you simply empty the cylinder of the empty shells and insert new ones. It's very simple and fast."

"I see that," said Nikolai. "I can see where this would be very effective. And the rifle is the same?"

"Not exactly. It doesn't have a cylinder. The shells are placed in a chamber. There's a bolt lever that you lift and pull back to empty a spent cartridge. When you push it back forward, it inserts a new cartridge into the chamber."

Stepan and Nikolai looked at each other in amazement.

"You'll spend some time on the firing range learning to use both."

"We hear you're working in the pharmacy," said Stepan.

Vasile smiled. "I supervise the inventory and oversee mixing the compounds."

"But don't you have to have a higher education to do that?" asked Nikolai.

"No, I don't blend the compounds. We have a pharmacist from the university who does that. I just oversee the inventory to make sure the chemicals are properly accounted for."

"Congratulations," said Nikolai.

Vasile grinned. "It's nice duty."

Vasile showed them around the post until it was time for lights out.

Chapter 20

After a week of training with the new weapons, Stepan, Nikolai, and four other soldiers were assigned to patrol the city. They spent ten hours a day on their horses. On the tenth day, they were policing the shore of the Black Sea.

"This is as bad as riding through the mountains," said Stepan.

Nikolai laughed. "Not quite. At least we have people to look at and it's much smoother, don't you think?"

Stepan smiled. "You know what I mean, Nikolai."

Nikolai nodded and smiled.

It was getting dark. Suddenly, Nikolai pulled back on his reins. "Hold up, men. I think I heard something. Be alert."

The sound of breaking glass crashed through the air followed by a commotion of voices.

"Follow me," ordered Nikolai. "Be at the ready."

The six of them advanced with caution. There was a crowd of about twenty men between two buildings. One of them saw the soldiers and alerted the others. The group watched Nikolai and his men approach.

"What's going on here?" asked Nikolai.

"We're having a discussion," said one of the men. He turned toward the others who laughed.

"Does your discussion include breaking glass?" asked

Nikolai.

"What does it matter to you? It's not your building," said another man. There was a murmur of agreement among the men.

"It's really of no matter to me, except it's an unlawful disturbance. I suggest you disband and go to your homes," said Nikolai.

"We'll go to our homes when we're ready. Why don't you mind your own business and go back to your post."

"Gentlemen, you must disband."

"Or what?"

Suddenly, several gunshots rang out. Aza moved in a panic and it took all of Stepan's strength to hold him. *Something's wrong with my leg!* Stepan felt a searing pain moving down his left leg and he felt a warm dampness on his pants. Looking down, he saw a patch of blood spreading. *I've been shot!*

He looked toward Nikolai, saw an empty saddle, and felt panic wash through him like a flood. He saw Nikolai lying on the street unmoving.

Trying to ignore the pain, he lifted his right leg over his saddle to climb down from Aza, but his wounded leg wouldn't hold his weight. Unable to stop himself, he slid down the side of his horse and landed face-first on the ground, his left foot caught in the stirrup. The pain was excruciating, but he strained to reach Nikolai.

A soldier was dabbing at a stream of blood coming from Nikolai's chest. Nikolai's head was on its side, tilted toward his feet, with his eyes trying to see Stepan. Blood drained from his mouth.

"Nikolai, can you hear me?" Stepan called.

Nikolai tried to nod.

Stepan stretched his hand toward Nikolai.

Nikolai tried to speak. There was a gurgle in his throat. More blood seeped from his mouth followed by a flow of air.

"Don't die, Nikolai! I need you!"

"He can't hear you, Stepan. It's too late," said the soldier as he closed Nikolai's eyes.

Stepan stared at Nikolai's face, which seemed strangely relaxed as blood trickled from his mouth. Stepan felt hot tears stream from his eyes. *Why, God? Why?*

Suddenly, Stepan was again aware of the pain in his leg. Two soldiers lifted him off the ground as another freed his foot from Aza's stirrup. He closed his eyes, gritted his teeth, and wept for Nikolai . . . and himself.

Chapter 21

Stepan stared at the dust particles floating in the streams of sunlight shining through the infirmary window. *God, how could you let this happen? I've lost two fathers. This is too much for me.* He was startled when the doctor spoke. "Stepan."

Stepan turned to him.

"How are you feeling this morning?"

Stepan shook his head.

"You won't have to have surgery. The bullet missed the bone. There's a nasty hole where it came out that will take some time to heal. You'll need to exercise as soon as you can, to strengthen your muscles so they won't shrink."

"When is Nikolai's funeral? Can I go?"

"Yes, they're waiting until you can be moved. You'll be carried on a cot and you'll have to lie flat in a wagon coming and going. If you give me your word that you won't try to walk, I'll allow it."

"Where's Aza?"

"Aza?" asked the doctor?

"My horse."

"With the rest of the horses, I suppose. You'll have to ask someone else. Will you give me your word?"

Stepan nodded.

"You didn't eat your breakfast. You need your nourishment.

Can I trust you to do all you can do to help yourself?"

"Yes," Stepan answered.

"Try to get some sleep now. It's the best thing for you."

When Stepan awoke it was dark. He opened his eyes to find Vasile sitting beside his bed.

"How are you doing, my friend?"

"Where's Aza?" asked Stepan.

'He's in his stall being well taken care of. How are you doing?"

"I'll survive, I suppose. I feel numb . . .. empty."

"I have some of Nikolai's personal things when you're ready for them."

Stepan furrowed his eyebrows. "What things?"

"A knife, a pocket watch, some money, a few photographs, and some other things."

"I'd like to see them," Stepan replied.

"I'll bring them in the morning."

"What about his rifle and pistol?"

"They belong to the army."

"His horse?"

"He belongs to you. The Commander said to give you everything else. Do you want Nikolai's horse?"

"I don't know, I'll think about it."

"He's being kept in the officer's stables for you."

A nurse walked up to the bed. "That's enough visiting," she said to Vasile. "You can come back tomorrow." She turned to Stepan, "Are you ready for some soup and bread?"

"I guess so," said Stepan. "I'm not very hungry."

"I'll come back tomorrow, Stepan." Vasile said, standing. "Eat." He leaned over the bed and whispered in Stepan's ear, "I love you, brother. We're family. I'll help you through this." He turned and left the infirmary.

"Do you have much pain?" asked the nurse.

"Only when I move."

"I can give you a little more medicine if you want . . . after you eat."

"No," said Stepan. "I want to get strong."

"The medicine will help you sleep. This is what your body needs more than anything now. I'll be back with your food."

After Stepan ate, the nurse returned and gave him some powder. "Place this under your tongue and let it dissolve. It'll be bitter, but it won't last long."

Stepan complied. He stared at the ceiling. Then his eyes closed. He thought of Nikolai and drifted off to sleep.

The funeral was short. The chaplain said some words about what a brave man Nikolai was . . . how he'd be missed by all who knew him. "Do you want to say some words, Stepan?"

What can I say? There are no words to express how I feel.

Stepan shook his head, tears streaming down his face.

The chaplain said a short prayer. Six soldiers placed the wooden coffin in the grave. Vasile handed Stepan a handful of dirt. Stepan tossed it in the hole.

The wagon ride back to the infirmary was bumpy, and Stepan groaned in agony every time the wagon bounced. To take his mind off the pain, he pulled out Nikolai's pocket watch. He wasn't interested in the time. He stared at the watch. It was gold and well taken care of. He'd seen Nikolai pull it from his pocket many times and polish it with a cloth. There was an inscription on the back, "Bold One." The chain was gold and heavy with a smaller chain attached to a gold toothpick. Nikolai had laughed and said, "This pick is worth more than all my teeth. I should sell it."

The wagon came to a stop. Two men carried Stepan into the hospital and put him back in bed. He was glad to be back.

"Do you want some medicine, Stepan?" asked the nurse.

Stepan nodded weakly.

Stepan walked as much as he could endure. He did everything he could to occupy his mind. *This is more than I can take. My father dies. I'm kidnapped. Nikolai dies. I'm wounded. I can't be with my family. I'm stuck in Odessa. We're killing Jews. I feel like I'm losing my mind.*

Chapter 22

Five weeks later, Stepan was released from the infirmary. "Let's go for a ride, Vasile. It seems like forever since I've ridden Aza."

He and Vasile rode their horses along the Black Sea. "Now that you're getting stronger, we can explore the city together. It's not all violence here. In fact, for the most part, it's become very peaceful."

"Do you miss being a Cossack, Vasile?"

Vasile stopped his horse. Stepan reined Aza to a halt.

"Are you kidding? Why would I? Don't tell me you do."

"I miss Nikolai and Aksay. It wasn't like we were raiding or fighting. It was peaceful. I enjoyed the school."

"That was nice, but it's in the past. We're here now—in Odessa, in the Russian Army. We have to make the best of where we are." Vasile spread his arms out gesturing toward the sea and the city.

"Are you happy?" Stepan pressed.

"Happy? What is happy? I make the best of where I am. Can I change anything? Can you?"

"No. I suppose not."

Vasile nudged his horse forward. Stepan prodded Aza.

"I know what you need, my friend. I can introduce you to a lady."

"That would be nice," said Stepan.

"Oh! So we've become a ladies' man now?"

"No, but I'm really tired of the army. I'd like some female companionship. Just for the conversation, something besides fighting talks."

"Come with me. I'll introduce you to Hilda and her sister Gertrude. You'll like them and their family. Not to mention the cooking."

The days passed faster for Stepan with the addition of a social life.

"I've been thinking," said Vasile, "How would you like it if I could get you assigned to the pharmacy with me?"

"You could do that?"

"I don't know that I can, but if you're interested, I'll recommend you to Aleksandr and tell him I want you there when there's an opening."

"I guess so. Doesn't it have to be earned?"

"Sometimes there are exceptions. Nikolai was well respected and he was your soldier. This will go a long way in your favor. Besides, you won't be any good to the police unit with that leg—at least not for some time."

Stepan pulled out his pocket watch and polished it. *You're still watching out for me, Nikolai.* He smiled to himself.

Three months later Stepan was assigned to work in the pharmacy.

"I still don't know how you did it, Vasile."

"I told you, I told headquarters I wanted you to work with me."

"I know, but one day you were just working in the pharmacy, next you're the supervisor, and now I'm working for you," Stepan wondered.

"You don't want it?"

"Of course, I do. It just amazes me. That's all."

"Good. You'll do what I did before I got promoted."

"You mean doing the inventory?"

"Yes, you're good at math and science. I didn't choose you just because you're my friend. However, you've told me that you want to be more than a soldier. This is an opportunity."

"Thank you. I'm grateful."

"That's more like it. You're welcome. You'll be working the evening watch starting next week. The pharmacist is Russo. He's from the university. I've already told him about you. And, by the way, the evening watch is much slower than the day watch. You won't be on your feet as much so your leg will heal faster." He winked at Stepan. "Now, let's get you started."

After a few weeks, Stepan was completely at home in the pharmacy.

"I think I have a knack for this," said Stepan, mostly to himself.

"You soldiers," grumbled Russo. "So, you think you have a knack for this? You think that's all it takes?"

"No, of course not, but you do make it look easy."

"Ha," spat Russo. "It looks easy only because I've spent hours studying all night and processing mixtures in the university laboratory all day for a long time."

"It's hard not to envy you," replied Stepan. "Maybe you'd consider teaching me."

"You must be a fool. Teach a soldier?" He spat on the floor." "I only do what I'm doing because I'd have to work for my father-in-law if I didn't. That'd be worse than working for Vasile."

Stepan's eyes narrowed as he studied Russo. "What's so bad with working for Vasile?"

Russo laughed. "You must be joking!"

"Not at all," replied Stepan.

"You soldiers think you can do everything, eh? You come into our city and kill anyone who speaks out. Who do you think you are? You think you're smarter than everyone, but you're not. Why would someone like Vasile be in charge of this pharmacy? What does he know about medicines? The only reason he's here is because he's a cold blooded-killer. He's some kind of hero. Everyone in the city is afraid of him. Don't take my word for it. Ask other soldiers. Ask any citizen on the street. They all know the name, Vasile the Killer."

Stepan's mind froze. Confusion rushed in and numbed him. *He can't be talking about Vasile!* His mind swirled. He swallowed hard. Clenching his fists, he stepped toward Russo.

Russo stepped back and smirked. "See how easily your anger is aroused? You're just like him!"

"No! I'm not!"

"Yes, you are. You soldiers are all alike. You don't care who you kill. I'd watch my back if I were you." Russo smirked.

Stepan awoke after a nearly sleepless night. Shaking his head, he tried to lose the thoughts. *Vasile's a killer. Watch my back . . . watch my back.*

He spent most of the day in the barracks, not wanting to face anyone. The weather matched his mood—dreary, rainy, and windy.

That night as Stepan walked to the pharmacy, the north wind blew against his back—pushing him. *Even the weather is against me.* He buried himself deeper into his fur coat, pulling the collar higher to keep the wind from blowing down his neck. Ducking his head, he pulled his heavy fur hat down tightly to cover his ears, and shoved his cold hands deep into his pockets. Snow pelted his back like tiny pieces of gravel. He hurried along the path toward the pharmacy. He was on the midnight watch.

His teeth chattered as a gust of wind whipped between two buildings, came out full force on the side of his face, and startled him out of his trance. His emotions swirled around like the snow. Beads of sweat popped out under his hat, but it wasn't the warmth of the hat that caused them.

Stepan pushed open the door of the pharmacy. He no sooner had stepped inside than . . . .

"Stepan, I want to talk to you. Come into my office . . . now!" ordered Vasile.

Stepan wondered at the tone of voice. Without hesitation, he stepped into Vasile's office. "What is it?" Stepan asked.

Vasile was sitting behind his desk, his hands clasped behind his head. "Something's happened. Something bad has happened!" His face belied the statement. "The pharmacy is being accused of distributing compounds that prevent men from being drafted into the army. What have you done?"

"What do you mean, what have I done?"

"I mean you've been distributing prescriptions and solutions to make men appear sick so they can avoid the draft! You're in serious trouble, you little fool. I've checked the log for the last several weeks. You're in charge of the inventory. Every entry showing the removal of the suspected elements has your name beside it! You've been a very naughty little boy."

Stepan's face burned hot with anger as Vasile's mouth twisted into a sneer. "You've used me!" Stepan said through gritted teeth. "The only reason you brought me here is to make me a pawn in your twisted scheme. You *are* a killer, aren't you?"

Vasile pulled his hands from behind his head and leaned forward. "So what if I am," he hissed. "Why did my mother get killed and yours didn't? And your friendship with Nikolai made me sick."

"What's happened to you?" retorted Stepan.

Vasile came out of his chair. He had a pistol in his hand. Deliberately he walked around the desk pointing the pistol at Stepan. "Nikolai isn't here to protect you now, you little Jew!

Do you think I brought you here because you're someone special, my friend?" Vasile spit at Stepan's feet. "Don't kid yourself. We were never friends. I could kill you myself, but the captain of the guard will be here any second to take you away in chains."

Slapping the pistol away with his left hand, Stepan shoved his right hand into Vasile's face, pushing him back onto the desk. Vasile's gun fired, sending a bullet into the ceiling. Turning, Stepan bolted out of the office.

"Fool! You're a dead man," yelled Vasile. He fired a wild shot toward Stepan.

Stepan pushed through the pharmacy door and into a wall of blowing snow. Papers whirled in a whirlwind of cold air behind him

Vasile ran to the door and fired three shots into the night. "You're a dead man, Stepan!" Vasile screamed. "A dead man!"

Chapter 23

Stepan raced through the blinding snow until he crashed into a wooden fence. The corral. He couldn't see anything, but used the fence to guide him to the barn. Once inside, he doubled over and breathed in warmer air. In minutes he had Aza saddled. He grabbed his rifle, sword, and pistol, but left his lance. *It'll just get in my way. I wish I had those repeating weapons.*

He led Aza through the barn door and threw himself into the saddle. "I hate to send you out in this blizzard," he told Aza. "But if we can't see anything, neither can they. Riding in the snow will be hard on you, but I'll rest you as often as I can."

Indecision clouded his thinking. *Aksay? No, don't be stupid. Think, Stepan, there's no room for fear.* He covered his mouth, breathed deep, and exhaled slowly. *Word of my desertion will spread like wildfire. Every soldier will be looking for me. Surely they heard the shots. I must be as far from Odessa as possible by daylight.*

He pulled his watch and compass from his pocket. Five hours until first light. *West . . . west . . . Moldova—through Moldova to Romania. Moldova is sparsely populated in the south and it will take me north of the three Russian soldier communities on the east border of Romania.* He pulled Aza around and headed west at a gallop. Leaning forward, Stepan whispered in Aza's ear, "We've been through much together, my friend, but this is for our lives. We'll gallop for a while and then I'll give you the reins. The snow will cover our tracks. What has happened, Aza? I feel like I'm losing my mind. Vasile has surely lost his. He's become a killer. He has betrayed me. What has he been doing?"

Stepan's mind churned, trying to put pieces together. *What did Vasile say? Distributing prescriptions and solutions to make young men appear sick so they can avoid the draft. Avoid the draft. Sick? So they can avoid the draft . . . avoid the draft?*

Stepan slumped in his saddle.

A hint of light began to creep across the sky. The blizzard had ended and now only a light snow fell. Stepan slowed Aza, pulled him off into a stand of trees, and listened to the sounds of the snowflakes falling among leaves. There were no other sounds except for Aza's breathing. He climbed off the horse, tied him to a tree, and kicked at the snow uncovering some grass.

"Here's some food for you, boy. I wish our lives were as peaceful as this grove, Aza. At least I have water."

He pulled his canteen from inside his coat, swallowed all the water, and refilled the container with snow. He put it back inside his coat so the warmth of his body would melt the snow. *I'll have to wait for food.* "We can stop for an hour, Aza, and then we have to move on. I can't sleep yet, but you need to rest."

An hour later, Stepan stared through his telescope in the direction they had come. The land sloped to the east and he searched as far as the snow allowed him, which wasn't far. *I'm glad the snow's still falling. It's as difficult for them to see as it is for me. I wish I knew how far we've come . . . if any soldiers are out there. The Dniester River is somewhere ahead. I'll feel better when we've crossed it. Maybe I can spear some fish. Meat would be wonderful, but rifle fire could give us away.*

It was nearly noon when they came to the river. The snow had stopped. Only deer and small game were visible. "I can't use my rifle, Aza. The sound will carry too far." They crossed the Dniester River. "We've got to eat and rest, Aza." After tying Aza to a tree, Stepan found enough grass under the snow to feed his horse. He searched the river and spotted some salmon. He then made a spear from a tree limb and stood patiently on the riverbank, searching for one close enough to spear. Within a few minutes, he had speared, filleted, and eaten one. Contented, he lay back in the sun.

Stepan awoke with a start, Aza's nose nudging his back.

"You're tired of standing in one spot, Aza?"

Stepan stood and stretched. *Snowing again—beautiful.* He checked his watch. It was nearly 2100. *The reality of his situation roared into his mind. It doesn't matter what time it is, I have to start moving. Even if the soldiers aren't behind me, the tsar's police probably are. Would Vasile report me to the Okhrana? Of course he would. The tsar's secret police will track me anywhere. The Okhrana!*

He saddled Aza, climbed into the saddle, and checked his compass. He nudged Aza west, let him have the reins, and snuggled into his coat for the night's ride. Thoughts drifted through his mind. A deeper thought began to emerge. *He wouldn't do that . . . send the Okhrana to Gagra? Momma! Israel! God, please don't let him do that! Vasile, why did you . . . why would you?*

The sun was brilliant as if it were saying good morning. He didn't know if he was still in Moldova or Romania—not that it really mattered. It wouldn't stop the soldiers, but he felt he would have a better chance of finding friendly people in Romania.

Something caught his eye. *Is that a cloud?* He inspected it through his telescope. *It's definitely smoke, but I don't see any buildings. The trees are too thick. It could be a campfire. Obviously, no one's trying to conceal it. If it's a farm, I may be close to a road. As tempting as it is to be in a warm house eating a hot meal, it's too dangerous . . . maybe further west.* He saw smoke several times in the next couple of days, but Stepan avoided all towns and farms.

Two days later, the snow was shallow enough in the woods that Aza found grass. Stepan's stomach growled. *I need food . . . and sleep. I'm surely in Romania by now.* He left Aza tied to a tree and surveyed the surroundings for any sign of food while moving in the direction of some smoke on the horizon. He topped a hill and saw a small clump of buildings in the valley ahead. His telescope revealed two houses, a blacksmith shop, and a store. *No movement. Should I bypass them? I need food and clothes. I've got to get rid of this uniform. This is probably as good a time as any to take a risk.*

"Would you like some oats, Aza?" He shifted the pistol in his belt, pulled his rifle out of the scabbard, and nudged Aza forward.

Stepan climbed out of his saddle and tied Aza to a post in front of the store. *Maybe they've never seen a soldier before. I have no choice.* He stepped into the store. The immediate warmth of the wood stove drew him. He stood there for several minutes enjoying its warmth, aware of three men watching him. They said nothing. He smiled at them and said in Low German, "I've been on the road for several days and have forgotten how good a wood stove feels."

"Would you like some coffee?' asked a man behind a counter, returning the smile.

He must be the owner. "Coffee would be very welcome."

"Where do you come from?"

"East."

"You're traveling through Romania this time of year? A man could get lost and never be found in this snow-covered country."

Stepan almost smiled. *Good, Romania.* "Snow's everywhere in Europe. Why would Romania be any different?"

Stepan leaned his rifle against a chair as the man approached him with a steaming cup. Accepting the mug with his left hand, he kept his right hand free just in case.

"Thank you," said Stepan. He sipped it and let the hot liquid slide down his throat. "Good."

"Where are you headed?" asked one of the others.

"South." *I hate to lie, but . . . .* He finished the coffee, picked up his rifle, and walked to a shelf holding several pair of pants. Leaning his rifle against the shelf, he took off his coat, and turned toward the men clearly exposing the pistol in his belt. He laid his coat on the counter. Shaking out a pair of wool pants, he held them up to him. They were too big. "Do you have a smaller size?"

The owner came over and pulled down another pair from the shelf. "These should fit."

"I'll need two pairs, two shirts, a heavy coat, a pair of heavy boots, and a hat. What food's available?"

"Beef and deer jerky, potatoes, raisins, nuts, and candy."

"Are you a bargaining man?"

"It depends on what's being offered."

"This Russian rifle. It should be worth these items and more."

The proprietor reached for the rifle. "Army?"

"It's a good one," said Stepan, slipping his right hand around the handle of his pistol. "You can do no better. Be careful, it's loaded."

The man looked Stepan in the eye as he lifted the rifle to his shoulder. He pointed it to a window and looked down the sights. He did this several times, checking the balance and the weight. The owner motioned the other two men over to him.

"It would make a fine hunting gun for deer," one man said smiling. "Do you have more ammunition?"

"Yes, outside."

The third man reached for the rifle and tested its balance. "You've used this in combat?"

Stepan ignored the question.

"What's fair to you, soldier?" asked the proprietor.

Stepan was surprised at the word. He thought for a moment. "The clothes, some beef jerky, potatoes, raisins, nuts, and some oats for my horse."

The owner raised his eyebrows. "You drive a hard bargain."

"I think I'm being more than fair. You know a good rifle when you see one," he said, nodding at the other two men. "I could ask for more."

"And I could offer less . . . we're agreed." He placed the clothes in one cloth sack, the food in another, and tied them together.

Stepan slung them over his shoulder, slid his hand around his pistol, and walked outside.

The three men followed him.

He threw the sacks over Aza's neck, reached in his saddlebags, and pulled out the bag containing the powder and balls. He handed them to the owner.

"I'm not sure who got the better bargain," said the second man.

Stepan nodded to the men, climbed on Aza, and nudged him south. He didn't look back. Once back in the trees, he turned Aza west.

Three hours west of the settlement, Stepan turned Aza into the woods and tied him to a tree. After removing Aza's saddle, brushing him down, and giving him some oats, Stepan changed clothes, started a fire, and burned his uniform. *It feels weird and wonderful to be free of that uniform.*

Stepan cut some strips of jerky and pushed a potato into the red coals with a stick. He chewed on the jerky while the potato cooked. "Not a bad meal, Aza. Do you like your oats? It feels good to have something decent in your stomach, doesn't it, boy? Me too."

Stepan took in a deep breath and let out a sigh. He laughed when Aza snorted. "You feel full too, boy?" Stepan checked the time—0900. "Time to get some sleep, Aza. It might be safe to travel by day now, but I don't want to risk it." A yawn slipped out. "Besides, I'm too tired to go on. I bet you are too."

He put more wood on the fire, pulled a blanket from his saddlebag, and curled up by the flames. "I don't how much longer we're going to be together, my friend. The old world is slipping away from us. What will our new world hold? "The smell of the fire caused his thoughts to drift back to his childhood—remembering the days he and his father went hunting and fishing, the smells of food his mother prepared, her warm embrace, the softness of his bed, the laughter of his little brother, and the night of terror that changed his life. *Will I ever see them again?* The thought haunted him. Sleep finally overtook his mind, but a terror- filled dream of the *Okhrana* robbed him of rest.

Stepan woke to Aza pawing the ground. *He's ready to go.* The moon light filtered through the bare trees. The fire had gone out. Checking the time, he was surprised that he'd slept for twelve hours. He sliced some jerky, put it in his coat pocket, and filled his canteen with snow. He climbed on Aza and eased him toward the road. No signs of movement in any direction so Stepan walked Aza out of the woods. He kicked Aza in his flanks and then gave him his head. "I've never seen you run this fast, boy. You must have really liked the oats." After a few kilometers, he pulled back on the reins. "Whoa, Aza, that's enough. We don't know our way through this country. We don't want to come upon someone or something too fast."

"I didn't know Romania was this desolate, Aza. We've been travelling by day for five days and not a sign of human life. Not that it would do us any good. There's nothing else to trade for food. I stretched my food as far as I could and now I'm hungry enough to eat your oats. I wish I hadn't sold my rifle, but I had no choice, did I? I'm getting weak. I don't think I can go another day on this empty stomach."

It was nearly dark when Stepan saw a light through the trees to his right. He brought Aza from a trot to a walk. *What have we here?* A lane appeared. "Whoa, boy." Stepan looked down the lane. *It looks like a farm.* Stepan could make out a fence and gate. Nudging Aza into the lane, he studied the layout. *A house, barn, corral.* The light was coming from a lamp just inside a window of the house. He climbed off Aza and opened the gate.

"Stay where you are!" a voice commanded.

Where is he? Stepan's eyes searched the house, but could see no one.

"Put your hands behind your head."

Stepan obeyed.

Two men with rifles stepped from the side of the house and walked to him. Stepan judged one to be in his late thirties and the other about ten years younger.

"Who are you?" asked the younger one. "And what do you want?"

"Food. I haven't eaten for three days."

"That's what you want, but I asked who you are."

"My name is Stepan Ivanov."

"Russian! A German speaking Russian travelling in Romania."

The younger man approached Stepan cautiously, opened Stepan's coat with the end of his rifle barrel, and focused on Stepan's pistol. "Move slowly and toss that pistol away from you."

Stepan did exactly as he was told.

"Now, step into the yard."

As Stepan obeyed, the older man took Aza's reins. He reached to the saddle, pulled Stepan's sword from its scabbard, and stuck it in the ground.

The sword! I should have buried it when I burned my uniform!

"What are you, boy, a thief or a coward? What's a Russian doing with a Cossack's sword travelling in Romania in the dead of winter?" asked the older man. "Never mind, I know the answer."

How could you know the answer?

"You're running. Why? From whom?"

Stepan didn't answer.

"Answer me, boy."

"He killed someone," said the younger man.

"No," said Stepan. "I was accused of a crime I didn't commit."

"That's all? And you ran?"

A third man stepped from the house. "Soldiers don't run. Neither do Cossacks. There must be more to your story than that."

God please help me.

The youngest man pushed his rifle against Stepan's belly. "Why did you run?"

"I was afraid for my life."

"Did you hear that, Father? He was afraid for his life."

"I heard. He can't help what he is." All three men stared at him.

"He's a coward."

Anger burned in Stepan's face.

"Leave him alone," said the third man.

"But . . . ."

"You heard me."

The younger man picked up Stepan's pistol and put it in his belt. "I want to study this gun. I've not seen one like it before."

Stepan winced at the loss of his weapon. He thought of his knife in his boot, but knew it would be of no benefit in this situation.

"Take your horse to the barn," the older man said to Stepan. "You can tend to him in the far stall. There are some oats in the corner."

Stepan could feel the men's stares as they followed him into the barn—studying every move. He removed Aza's saddle and bridle, brushed him down, and poured some oats for him. Turning toward the three men, he said, "I can only place myself in your shoes. It's an uncertain situation, but I'm not a threat—I'm just trying to survive."

"It's only you who is in an uncertain situation. You're a Russian soldier in Romania, dressed like a Romanian, speaking German. Did you think you'd find friends here?" asked the middle man.

"I had hoped," replied Stepan, dropping his head.

"We'll sort this out later," said the older man.

"But, we need to know who he is" cried the younger man.

"You heard me. We have his weapons, except for the knife in his boot." The older man looked Stepan in the eye. "Do you think I cannot see, boy? Toss it on the ground."

Stepan lifted his right leg, pulled the knife from his boot, and tossed it on the ground.

The younger man immediately picked it up. "Nice knife," he said, smiling as he shoved it in his belt.

Stepan was too weak and tired to worry any more. He slumped against the rail of the stall.

"Get him some food."

"We should let him starve, Father."

"He can sleep in the loft for now. If he tries to escape, we'll shoot him."

Chapter 24

Stepan woke with the sun shining on his face through the slits in the barn roof. Although he could see his breath, the hay was warm. His coat served as a blanket and kept him comfortable. He checked his watch. It was past noon. He climbed down from the loft. "I think we may be in trouble, Aza."

He walked to the barn door and surveyed the area. There was no one in sight. As soon as he stepped through the door, the middle man stepped out of the house. He didn't have a rifle, but Stepan could see a pistol in the man's belt. He motioned Stepan to come to him.

He was tall, muscular, and clean shaven with long brown hair. His skin was weathered. He eyes watched Stepan closely.

"I've been instructed to bring you to the house to eat. If it were up to me, I'd run you off." He stepped aside and let Stepan go by.

Stepan opened the door and walked into a warm kitchen with a fireplace in the corner. It smelled of freshly baked bread and stew, reminding him of home. The other two men were sitting at the table.

"Sit," said the older man to Stepan. "Bring him a dish of stew," he instructed the younger man.

The younger man let out a heavy sigh, pushed his chair

back, and stomped toward the fireplace. A moment later, he set a bowl of stew in front of Stepan, sloshing some on the table. He pushed a plate of bread forward. Stepan caught the plate just as it slid off the table.

"Good reflexes," said the older man.

A girl stepped into the room, went to the stove, and poured a cup of steaming coffee. She set it on the table in front of Stepan, turned, and left the room.

She's beautiful He caught himself, aware of the three men staring at him intently.

"Eat," said the older man. "Then we'll talk."

Stepan took a spoonful of the stew and wolfed down a large bite of bread. As he finished the stew, the older man spoke.

"If I were to let you go, where would you go from here?

"I'm not sure, I don't know exactly where I am," replied Stepan. "West, I suppose."

"You have no plan?"

"Just to find a safe place."

"Where did you get the clothes?"

"At a settlement five days east."

"How did you pay?"

"I traded my rifle."

"Traded your rifle?" the older man questioned.

"Yes."

"Aye. If the Russians are following you, they'll know they're on the right trail."

"I had no choice. I needed food and I didn't want to keep

wearing my soldier uniform. I had very little money . . . not enough to pay for what I needed."

"What did you do with your uniform?"

"I burned it and buried the ashes."

"That was wise," agreed the older man. "And you said it was five days ago." He stroked his chin. "It's done and can't be changed. We'll keep a sharp watch. In the meantime, I want to know how it is that you're running from the Russians."

"It's as I told you, I was accused of a crime I didn't commit."

"I know what you told me, but it tells me nothing. You have put us at risk. I deserve to know more."

"Yes, I suppose you do. It was a betrayal . . . " Stepan told a few details of his escape.

The older man studied Stepan's face for several moments before he spoke. "I sense you're telling me the truth, but I think there's more. Did anyone follow you?'

"No."

"How do you know?"

"I stopped three hours west of the settlement and slept."

"You slept that close! That was very risky."

"Aza would've heard anyone approaching."

"Aza's your horse?"

"Yes."

"You trust your horse that much?"

"This man is either very brave or he's a fool," said the younger man.

Stepan stared at the table. *What are they going to do with me?*

"I like you, boy," said the older man. "You have courage. You said your name's Stepan?"

"Yes."

"Well, Stepan, this is my youngest, Petre. This is Serghei, my oldest. I'm Ferka."

Stepan nodded.

"You boys get back to work," commanded Ferka. "I'm sure Stepan realizes his circumstance here. I want to get to know him better."

The two younger men left the house.

Ferka stared at Stepan for several moments. "Stepan, you're a mystery. You've endangered my family, yet I sense you aren't a threat. Those you're running from may be another matter. Our protection is to keep you here, at least until we're sure you haven't led anyone to us."

"I haven't led anyone to you," replied Stepan.

"Maybe yes, maybe no. We'll watch for a few days and see if anyone comes looking. If someone comes, we'll hide you, but we'll listen carefully to their story. If there are discrepancies, I'll decide what to do."

"But, they won't know the details. Their story will be distorted. They'll only know what they've been told." Stepan cried.

"Then tell me, why did you run?"

Stepan grudgingly told Ferka the details of the night of the escape.

"You've been through a lot, Stepan. Do you know why he did this to you? It seems strange that a friend would do such a thing."

"I've thought about this many times during my escape. The Russian Army was drafting local men to replace their heavy casualties. There were many prospects who were not in a condition to pass the two required physicals. I think Vasile was selling illegal compounds to make them ill enough to fail the exams."

"Very risky business," replied Ferka. "So you were the scapegoat."

"I think so."

"Now we must wait to see if someone comes looking for you. In the meantime, you can work for your keep. This is fair, is it not?"

"Yes, very fair."

"It takes hard work to feed a family of five and now you. We'll keep you busy. You can take care of the animals while my sons and I maintain our equipment and prepare for our spring sowing. In exchange, we'll feed you and your horse well. We have pigs and cattle that need to be tended to. Can you milk a cow?"

"I haven't milked a cow since I was a little boy, but I'm sure I can."

"Well, in the morning we'll go to the barn and see."

The girl and a woman came into the kitchen as if on cue.

"Is it time to prepare supper already? This is my wife and my daughter, Stepan. We call my wife Momma. My daughter's name is Rachael."

Momma! Stepan stood up and bowed. He felt his heart

pounding fiercely, his body trembling, and his face turning hot.

"The young man has manners," said Ferka.

Stepan couldn't speak.

"What's wrong, Stepan?" asked Ferka.

"I . . . I called my mother Momma," said Stepan dropping his eyes to the floor. "It's been a while since I've seen her."

The next morning Stepan stared at the rows of cows and sighed. He milked and fed the cows until noon. All afternoon he cleaned out the barn. He was exhausted at supper.

"You seem to be able to handle the cows, Stepan," said Ferka, smiling.

"I'm not sure I can hold my fork," replied Stepan. "I milked one cow when I was a boy. Forty cows is very different. I've never worked this hard. My hands feel like they might fall off."

The family laughed.

"We're not laughing because your hands hurt, Stepan," said Ferka. "We'll see if we can help those hands after supper."

After the table was cleared, Rachael sat down beside Stepan with a bowl partially filled with a thick substance and a rag. She reached out, took his hand, and covered it with a salve. She gently rubbed in the ointment. She looked into his face, smiled, and said, "This will make your hands feel much better."

Even though his hands hurt, the beating of his heart stopped him from feeling the pain. Her touch had a strange and wonderful affect on him.

"You're a hard worker, Stepan," said Ferka.

Stepan jumped. He'd forgotten everyone except Rachael.

"You never planned on this when you came through our gate, did you?" said Serghei.

I'm sure he's not referring to Rachael.

"No, my hands are angry with me," Stepan said, laughing.

A month later, Stepan's hands had toughened and were much better. The kitchen table had become his favorite place. He sat down in his usual place and immediately Rachael placed a fresh cup of coffee in front of him.

"A *gut morgn*, Rachael" said Stepan in Yiddish.

"A *gut morgn*," replied Rachael.

The rest of the family's conversation stopped immediately. Ferka stood up, his chair falling backwards. Momma dropped a bowl of potatoes. It shattered as it hit the floor.

"You speak Yiddish?" exclaimed Ferka.

"Don't be afraid," Stepan said in Yiddish. "I'm not an enemy, I'm a Jew."

"I should kill you right here and now," cried Petre. "There's no way we can know the truth about you."

"Quiet, Petre," yelled Ferka.

A hush fell over the kitchen.

It seemed forever before Ferka spoke. "Why do you think we're Jews?"

"You have pigs. You butcher, smoke, and hang them in your meat shed, but you don't eat them. Not at any meal."

Ferka sat back down. He ran his fingers through his hair.

"Sit down everyone."

Everyone sat. Ferka stared at Stepan and Stepan stared back unwaivering. Finally Ferka spoke.

"Tell us how we can know you're telling the truth, Stepan."

"When I was sixteen, the Cossacks raided my village . . . " Stepan told the entire story and waited for Ferka to respond. He was surprised when Rachael spoke first.

"I believe him, Father. The details of his story may be different than ours, but his circumstance is the same."

Ferka looked into Stepan's eyes. The silence was loud. "I believe you, Stepan," said Ferka softly.

"Father!" exclaimed Petre.

"Quiet, Petre. Stepan, it seems as though you have exposed a weakness in our charade. This is a good thing to know."

Stepan looked around the room. Petre was scowling and staring at him. Serghei showed no emotion while staring at the floor. Momma stooped down to pick up the pieces of the broken bowl. Rachael looked at him intently.

"You may stay as long as you wish," said Ferka.

Petre left the table and went outside slamming the door behind him.

Ferka went after him.

Stepan looked at Rachael. She smiled at him. He blushed.

Rachael and her mother finished clearing the table.

"I'm afraid the food isn't as hot as it was, but it'll still taste good," said Momma. "Please help yourself, Stepan. You're still our guest."

Stepan spooned some eggs on his plate and passed the

bowl to Serghei.

"Thank you, Stepan," said Serghei. He nodded and smiled.

Good. I hope this is a sign he's accepted me.

The door opened and Petre came in followed by Ferka. No one spoke. Both men took their places at the table. Ferka looked at Petre and nodded.

"I'm sorry, Stepan," said Petre. He looked Stepan in the eyes. "I saw you as a threat to our safety. I thought you were surely a spy sent by the Imperial Army. My fear overtook my reason."

"I understand, Petre. I've experienced that myself. We're alike."

"Good. Now let's eat and get to work," said Ferka. "We can talk later."

That evening after supper, Ferka called the family into the living room. After they were seated, Ferka looked into Stepan's eyes. "Is Stepan your real name?"

"No. It's Nathan . . . Nathan Hertzfield."

"A Jewish name indeed. It's a good name. There's nothing stopping you from using your real name now, is there?"

"No, I suppose not."

"Good," said Ferka, "we'll call you Nathan."

Nathan nodded, savoring the sound of it. He smiled, then a frown crept over his face.

"What is wrong?" asked Ferka.

"Nathan is a little boy. I am no longer he. I have grown

into a man. A Cossack. A Russian soldier. Stepan is a man."

"I understand your conflict. Here is something to think about. The *Okhrana* is looking for Stepan. Am I right?"

"Yes."

"They are not looking for Nathan. Sooner or later, you are going to have to change your name or risk your name causing your capture."

Squinting his eyes, Stepan stroked his chin. Anger flooded his face. "I'm free and yet I'm still trapped."

"Give yourself some time. We'll continue to call you Stepan. You'll know what to do when the time comes."

Taking a deep sigh, Stepan nodded.

Ferka changed the subject. "As you've guessed, we're Jews. We escaped from Poland. There are many Jews in Romania. Some of us are estate managers for a landlord. This can cause much friction with the Romanians."

"A lot of friction," said Petre. "We owned a large amount of land in Warsaw. During the peasant revolt last year, rural rioters made a special point of attacking Jewish landowners."

Stepan shifted in his chair.

"Death was certain," said Ferka, "so we escaped and came here only to find the same situation."

"Death?" asked Stepan.

"It would have been except we were helped by other Jews who came before us, who knew us, and were already established with the one who employs us. We were extremely fortunate."

"How did you find them?" asked Stepan.

"Much the same way as you," said Rachael. "That's why I said your circumstance is like ours. We came to a farm in desperation. We felt we had nothing to lose. We were greeted with guns and suspicion, but the elder recognized Father." Tears fell from Rachael's eyes.

The room was silent.

Ferka said, "After a few weeks, we were given this farm to manage. The landlord is a very powerful man and holds the mortgages on hundreds of homes, farms, and businesses. If any harm were to come to us, he would pull the mortgage of those involved. This is how he keeps things in check. Should I break the relationship with him, he would not hesitate to kill me . . . and my family."

Stepan nodded.

"The reason we raise pigs is to give us cover. The owner sells the meat to a settlement south of here. You're a great lesson for me. I didn't anticipate a Jew coming to me who might be a Russian soldier."

Stepan nodded.

"You've proven your worth," said Ferka.

"I've been thinking." Stepan looked at his hands. "I think I can be of more value to you. I'm an excellent marksman."

"Ah, you could bring us deer and small game. I'm limited to what I can pay above your room and board. My employer is more than frugal. I'll give you what I can."

Stepan smiled. "I've another idea. I could hunt game, as you suggested, give you part of it in payment for my room and board, and sell the rest. Would this be possible? I mean, would your landlord object to this?"

"I think that is a grand idea, Stepan." Ferka reached out his hand. "Shall we seal the agreement?"

"Does Stepan have to continue sleeping in the loft, father?" asked Rachael.

"He can sleep on the floor in front of the fire. Will this be all right, Stepan?

Stepan nodded. He dared not look at Rachael.

Chapter 25

Over the next several months, Stepan worked hard. Slowly but surely, he and Ferka developed a strong relationship. They had many conversations over chess games. They were evenly matched. The meal- times were filled with tasty foods and laughter. May rolled around quickly.

One evening, Stepan was winning a hard fought game of chess. Ferka said, "Stepan, we've spent much time together. You've worked harder than I expected. There's a question I've desired to ask you."

"What is it?"

"Are you familiar with the Pale of Settlement?"

"Yes, it's a section of land along the western border of Imperial Russia where Jews are allowed to live."

Ferka studied Stepan's face for a moment.

"The concentration of Jews in the Pale made them an easy target for massive anti-Jewish riots that often devastated whole communities." Ferka paused and looked Stepan directly in the eye for several seconds. "Perhaps you were part of such atrocities?"

He is still testing me. Stepan shook his head. "I'm familiar with the Pale, but I've never been there. I've only been in Georgia, Russia, Ukraine, and now here. Ferka, you may find this hard to believe, but in the years I was a Cossack, I killed one man, a Turk. I've never molested women or children."

"How could a Cossack not be a part of those things?" asked Petre.

"It may seem strange to you, but my captor and I became very close—like father and son. He protected me and kept me from raids until he was afraid it would become obvious to the others, which would have been dangerous for us both. I was the only child he kidnapped. He felt he had to for his own survival."

Ferka stood and walked to the door. He looked out the door for a long time.

Stepan almost spoke, but checked himself.

Ferka continued. "I protected my family as best I could. Then the Russians started tightening their control. I was a well-known businessman. They were trying to force me to give up my property. I also employed a number of Jews. They wanted me to eliminate them and hire Russians. It was hard enough to let my help go, but to hire Russians—I just couldn't do it."

"Ferka, you don't need to continue," said Momma, pulling Stepan from his thoughts.

Ferka smiled at her softly.

"Yes. Most of those escaping went to Germany. I didn't think that was best, so I decided to bring my family south to Romania. I didn't think there would be many Jews here, but even so, I felt it would be safer than going to Germany. It was difficult at first. We left with only the belongings we could carry. I got my wife, my children, and my mother out of the

Pale first, under the cover of darkness, and then, as difficult as it was, I walked away from my business, my land, and brought my family here. The tsar's secret police make such a thing very dangerous so we had to change our identity. My mother died of influenza the second year we were here. She's buried behind the barn."

"I'm sorry, Ferka." *I wonder how many families like this one I've helped tear apart. I feel terribly ashamed. I must put this behind me and leave it there. It'll have no place in my new life. Tonight I'll dream of having a home like this . . . a wife . . . children.*

Ferka nodded. "I'm grateful she lived long enough to see something other than the Pale."

"Ferka, may I ask you a question?"

"Of course."

"What is it like to be a father?"

Ferka's eyes became moist. He looked at Stepan for a moment and then smiled. "I'm not sure I can explain it to you. You have asked a very good question and you deserve a satisfactory answer. It's the most rewarding life a man can have. I see myself in my children--my mannerisms, my values. Seeing them is like seeing a reflection of me. Of course, it's mixed with the characteristics of my wife. She is a wonderful woman—an extension of me. I could not possibly be a good father without her. She came willingly from the Pale without knowing what lay in store for us. She trusted me. She knew I thought it would have to be better than life there, no matter how hard it might be. But now . . . "

"Now, I've made it dangerous for you again."

"Some, but not threatening. You actually made us more secure by uncovering a weakness we didn't realize existed. We didn't think of a Cossack being a Jew."

"I'm not the only one," said Stepan.

"I believe you, but we were unaware. Thank God, you're who you are. If you weren't and you uncovered our secret, it would have been disastrous."

"I don't understand, Ferka."

"Jews from here have formed a secret route to smuggle those escaping from Poland to Bucharest."

Stepan sat quietly for several moments. "A secret route to Bucharest?"

"Yes, people like me, property managers, who have the ability to provide food, lodging, money, and information for those who are escaping persecution."

"There must be a tremendous amount of risk for you and the others," said Stepan. "You cannot possibly know that everyone who comes through can be trusted."

"This is true. Occasionally a traveler stops, who wasn't sent and asks for food. We give them what they need and send them on. This was our intent with you, but with you . . ."

"I just happened to come to the right farm?"

"Let's give credit to God," said Ferka. "Only God knows why he directed you to our farm."

"I'm grateful," said Stepan. "How does one escape from here?"

"You'll know what you need to know when it's time. As I told you, my landlord owns a substantial number of properties. He is in league with others. None of them knows of this nor would they care. They're only interested in money. They only know we're Jews—hard workers and trustworthy. Any of my sons would be automatically hired for a farm, if I asked, and anyone I refer would be hired without question."

"I'm amazed how it's kept so secret," said Stepan.

"We have our ways," said Ferka.

"Ways?"

"I think you understand," said Ferka, tilting his head and raising his eyebrow. "If you were to go any direction but west you wouldn't get far. You're not in Russia now. This is our part of the country. We do what we have to do to maintain our secrecy. No one would ever find you."

Stepan stared at Ferka. "You would kill me?"

"Yes. You do understand why we would have to?"

"To protect yourselves and keep your secret."

Ferka nodded.

"Would it be Petre?"

"It would be any of us. We all have much to protect."

"Rachael . . . or Momma?" asked Stepan, his eyebrows rose. "They would kill?"

"If there was no man here to do it. Many lives would be at stake—ahead of us and behind."

Both men were silent for a while.

Stepan broke the silence, changing the subject. "I dream of being a father and having a family. My memories of my family life cause me to miss it greatly. Being with your family these last few months has made it even harder. I've seen your family praying, working, playing, and laughing together. It has created a tremendous desire in me to have this kind of life."

"Are you thinking of Rachael?"

Stepan was surprised at the question.

"I've seen the way you look at each other. Do you deny it?"

"No, I won't deny that I have strong feelings for her."

"I'd be disappointed if you didn't, Stepan. What I'm going to say will be hard for you to accept, but say it I must. I've no doubt you would make a fine husband and son-in-law . . . however it's far too dangerous. You're a hunted man. It would be difficult to protect her. "

"I would protect her with my life, Ferka . . . even from the *Okhrana*."

"I know you would, Stepan, but you talk as though the *Okhrana* is the only threat.

Stepan listened carefully.

The reason my sons are still here is because they understand there is safety in numbers. One man to protect two beautiful women is risky. I'd not be able to defend them from a man who has less than honorable intentions. Do you understand what I'm saying?

Stepan nodded.

My sons talk often of another land. They both should have a woman of their own. They're of age, but we all chose to interrupt our own escape to help others. We've had some very beautiful young ladies pass our way. I've seen both of them looking with hopeful eyes, but so far they've chosen to stay here with their mother and me. You're heading into dangerous territory."

Stepan leaned forward.

You traveling alone is one thing, but being accompanied by a beautiful young woman increases the danger and risk. Many would kill you for such a prize as Rachael, without giving it second thought. You've lived with the Cossacks to know what some men will do to a woman."

Stepan frowned. "I understand." Stepan's mind flashed back to Aksay and all the women there who were taken in raids to be Cossack wives. He shuddered at the thought of such a thing happening to Rachael. "You're like a father to me, Ferka. My father died when I was fifteen. How I miss him! Nikolai was like a father, but we never really discussed women. Does a man ever get over the need for a father?"

"No, I don't think so, Stepan. I think of mine often. I regret that my sons didn't know him. I share with them my memories, which are few. I was too young to really know him. I believe this is one of the reasons I'm so close to my sons. I want them to know me. You see how we work together."

"Yes," laughed Stepan. "I would not want to be an enemy. It was hard enough as it was."

"We do have enemies, but we are willing to risk helping others who are escaping persecution. Not all are as fortunate as we are. We know there could be risk to us, but we decided as a family that this is what we wanted to do."

Stepan frowned.

"What's bothering you?" asked Ferka.

"I've been here for five months and I haven't seen anyone come through."

Ferka was quiet for a moment before responding. "This is because we weren't sure of you."

"Still?"

"No, we are now, but we've had to be careful. We placed a signal up the road, and those escaping bypassed us and went to the next farm."

"A signal?"

"We have ways. It might be best if you don't know."

Stepan frowned. "I've caused you a lot of trouble."

"Yes, we didn't know what to do with you at first. We couldn't kill you for fear there were others and we couldn't let you go for the same reason. Now we know you're a hunted man. They haven't tracked you, but it doesn't mean they won't eventually be successful. You have thought of this, haven't you?"

"I suppose it's in my mind. It's just so peaceful here that I've pushed it to the back of my mind."

"That can be dangerous. The people who are after you don't give up."

Stepan shuddered. "I'm sorry, Ferka. I had no intention of bringing you harm."

"Such is our life. We are at risk no matter what we do. We've learned much from you. You've actually made us safer.

We are watching even closer now and will continue to do so long after you've gone."

A shudder went through Stepan. "What you've told me is a very well-kept secret. I had never heard of anything like it until you told me. If it were even rumored among the Russians, I'd have heard of it. News about such a thing would have traveled fast. Being in Romania would not have helped you. The *Okhrana* would infiltrate and would eventually expose your system."

"It's always a possibility, but we continue to learn, just like we've learned from you. God will forgive us if we eat some pig if we feel it's necessary."

"I understand. I had to eat bacon to keep my identity hidden in Russia."

"Any problem with your identity can be solved in Bucharest. We have someone there who can make new papers for you."

"I thank you for this information, Ferka. Now I know there's safety somewhere ahead. I will think on my new identity."

"Let me caution you. Bucharest is very dangerous. You will not want to stay there long. You will be given instructions where to go from there. Only God knows what is ahead of you."

Chapter 26

The next day after his chores were done, Stepan found his way to one of the fields that had been sown. The sun shone brightly, the birds sang cheerily, and the wind blew slightly from the south. He headed to a large boulder at the north end and climbed on top. Scanning the field, he assured himself that no one was around. He leaned back and let the full force of the sun warm his face.

He directed his mind back to all that Ferka had told him. *I could stay here and have a life with Rachael, if she'd have me, and let Ferka be my father; but what of the Okhrana? I've endangered these people enough. Would Rachael go with me? Ferka would never let her go.*

"It's time for me to go," Stepan said aloud.

"How far is it to Bucharest?" asked Stepan at supper.

"It's a five-day journey," replied Ferka. "Are you thinking of leaving?"

"Not because I want to, but I feel it's time. I'll leave in the morning."

Rachael ran from the table.

Stepan's eyes dropped to the floor.

Everyone at the table was quiet.

Ferka broke the silence. "Tonight will be a sad night for

us." He looked down at his boots. "Doing it quickly is the best way. You'll go to the Dambovita River. It comes from the Fagaras Mountains. Follow it into Bucharest. Once you get into the city, find your way to the Choral Temple. Ask someone in that area to direct you to the blacksmith. Show him this," Ferka handed Stepan a gold coin. "This is your passport from Bucharest on. The blacksmith will buy Aza and your saddle."

"Buy Aza? I don't want to sell him."

"You can't take him with you. From there you'll go by train."

"Can't Aza ride on the train? I'm sure there must be a way." Stepan stood.

"Not for you. Vasile knows your horse. Don't you think he's told the *Okhrana* about him—described him? You know he has. You cannot afford to draw attention to yourself. Loading a horse would be unusual."

Stepan buried his head in his hands.

"Just being one of the passengers is the safest way for you . . . and probably for Aza."

Stepan let out a heavy sigh. "Is there any end to this?" he mumbled.

Ferka gave him a moment.

"The blacksmith will also take care of any identification papers you'll need. Don't expect to receive a fair value. He not only must make a profit to sustain himself, but he accumulates funds to help the less fortunate on their journey as well. "

"Then where will I go?"

"I don't know. He will give you directions. We'll say our good-byes in the morning."

It seemed like forever before Stepan dropped off to sleep. A parade of faces went through his mind—each turning to vapor.

Breakfast was quiet. Rachael's place was noticeably empty. Stepan looked for her during the meal. No one mentioned her name.

"I'd enjoy nothing more than having you stay with us, Stepan," said Ferka, "but we both know it's dangerous. We've taken a great risk the last few months. We'll remember each other as we are now."

"I'll write you when I can."

"You can't, Stepan. It's too dangerous. We don't trust the mail."

"Then how . . . ?"

"There is no way, Stepan."

Stepan nodded and rose from the table. He hugged Petre, Serghei, and Momma and then he and Ferka walked to the barn.

"Here are your wages. I hope they're sufficient."

"I expected none," said Stepan. "My earnings were from the game I killed and you sold for me."

"It isn't enough for the work you've done. Use it in good health." He handed Stepan a sack. "Momma has packed enough food for your journey. Your knife is in the sack."

"Thank you, Ferka; you're indeed a generous man."

"Here's something else. You may want this." Ferka tossed Stepan's pistol to him.

Stepan grinned as he inspected it. "It's good to have it back." He slipped the pistol in his belt.

"You're a unique man, Stepan. You'll find a good woman and make a fine husband and father. Your trip to Bucharest will allow you to think over your experience with us. It will serve you well in your new home."

Stepan nodded. "Good-bye, friend."

"Good-bye," replied Ferka.

The two men hugged. Stepan climbed into his saddle. He turned to look at the house and searched for Rachael's face. It wasn't there. Turning his horse, Stepan rode toward the gate. Looking back, he waved to Ferka. He didn't look back again.

As he neared the gate, he heard a rustling in the trees to his left.

"Stepan! Stop!"

He pulled Aza to a halt.

Rachael stepped to the edge of the road.

Stepan looked behind him. There was no sign of Ferka. He nudged Aza into the trees and climbed down.

Rachael walked to him and stood so close he could feel the warmth of her body.

"You don't have to say anything, Stepan. I see how you feel in your eyes. Can you see how I feel?"

"Yes, Rachael, I wish things were different."

She threw her arms around his neck and pressed her lips on his. Her cheeks were wet with tears. She then placed her lips to his ear and whispered, "Take me with you."

His heart was pounding hard. His emotions were nearly out of control. "I can't, Rachael. I want to badly, but I can't. Another time, another place, and . . . "

She placed her finger on his lips. "Shhh . . . I know. I understand. Will you come back for me?"

"God knows I want to . . . but no . . . It can't be." Bending his face to hers, he kissed her softly. Her warm tears against his cheek tore at him. He turned toward Aza, stepped into the stirrup, and swung into the saddle. Looking down, his eyes locked with hers. Stepan forced a smile and nudged Aza through the gate. He rode a few feet, stopped, and looked back.

Rachael held one hand over her mouth and slowly waved with the other.

Stepan waved, turned, and rode away. *I'll miss you, Rachael, my love.*

All day long Stepan wrestled with himself. "I don't know what to do, Aza. I'm divided between going ahead and turning back. What could be better ahead of us than what we had at Ferka's? It's been months since we ran from Odessa. There's been no sign of the *Okhrana*. Not one Russian soldier. Is there really any danger or is it all in my head? How many times do I have to go through this? Momma and Israel, Nikolai, Rachael . . . if I keep going I'll be losing you, too."

Aza's reins were hanging loose. He seemed as sad as Stepan. He plodded along the road, his head bobbing up and down with each step.

Chapter 27

That night he camped alongside a lazy creek. Stepan lay on his blanket staring at the starlit sky. The moon was full. *Rachael, are you looking at the stars and thinking about me? I can still taste your lips. I feel your tears . . . hear your voice . . . see your lovely face. If I came back for you, would you still go with me? Even so . . . Ferka would never bless us. Would he and your brothers come after us?*

After a week, Stepan arrived at Bucharest in the late afternoon. The bustling city lay on both sides of the river. He surveyed the city. "We better find Choral Temple, Aza."

Once Stepan arrived at the temple, he had no problem locating the blacksmith Ferka had told him to talk to.

"Aza, I don't know if I can do this. We've been friends a long time. We've seen much together. It'll be strange and lonely without you. I don't know if I have it in me."

After a few moments, he tied Aza to a post and walked inside. The blacksmith was bending over a horseshoe hammering mightily. Stepan waited until he completed his task. Looking up, the blacksmith studied Stepan for a minute.

"What do you need?" he asked in Romanian.

Stepan guessed at what he said and responded in Yiddish. "I have a horse and saddle to sell. I was wondering if you might be interested in them."

The blacksmith stood up. He responded in Yiddish, "Why would I be interested? I sell horses, not buy them."

"This may interest you," Stepan showed him the gold coin.

The blacksmith nodded. "I'm busy. Come back later."

"How much later?"

"Have you found a place for the night?"

"No," Stepan answered.

"A short distance up the road is the Inn on the River. Go get your room and have supper. Come back after six o'clock. I'll be closed. Leave your horse with me."

"Why should I leave my horse?"

"If this is an issue of trust, you were a fool to show me the coin. It's worth much more than your horse, maybe even more than your life. It's better for you to leave your horse now. It would appear you left him for me to shoe. To come with him after I'm closed and leave without him would look suspicious. Either leave him or don't come back tonight."

Stepan nodded. He untied Aza, led him into the shop, and started to untie his bed roll.

"Just leave everything. If you have any personal items in your saddlebags, put them in your satchel. You won't need anything else. The money you have, put in your pocket, but what I give you, in your boot."

Stepan did as instructed.

"I'm not familiar with the currency here or the language."

"Because of the train there are people from many countries.

It'll be good that you know nothing and ask questions. Do you speak German?

"Yes."

"It is a good language to use. Don't let that coin be seen," the blacksmith warned.

Stepan nodded. He put his arms around Aza's neck. The horse nuzzled his nose against Stepan's head. Stepan turned to leave.

"Wait. When you come back knock on the door twice, wait a moment, and knock twice again."

Stepan left for the inn. *God, this has to be the last good-bye. I don't think I can take any more.*

Later that evening, he knocked twice on the blacksmith's door, paused, and then knocked twice again. The door opened and he entered.

"How was your meal," asked the blacksmith, "and your room?"

"The meal was excellent and the room is very comfortable."

"Good. Let's talk. I'll give you one hundred thousand leu for your horse and saddle."

Stepan put the money in his boot without counting it.

"What identification do you have?"

"Russian military."

The blacksmith raised his eyebrows. "Russian military identification?" The blacksmith shook his head in amazement. "I'd like to know your story, but it's best if I don't. Where are you coming from?"

The fear of exposing Momma and Israel immediately came to his mind. "Ukraine," Stepan replied.

"You found your way to the system from Ukraine? How did you find out about it? This is disturbing."

"I didn't find out about it there. There's no danger."

"Then how . . . no, I don't want to know. I'll destroy your papers in my fire. Your past life no longer exists. I'll need a name for your papers."

Stepan hesitated.

"You don't have a name?"

"Ivan . . . Ivan Popov."

"Come back in the morning at seven o'clock and I'll have your papers ready for you."

Stepan nodded and looked around. He didn't see Aza.

A knock on the door awakened Stepan from a sound sleep. "It's the time you requested, sir."

"I'm awake. Thank you."

It was still dark. He washed, shaved, and dressed. Descending the stairs, he could smell strong coffee and a mixture of food odors. He found a table by a window and looked out into the darkness.

A young woman approached him with a steaming cup of coffee. "You wish breakfast, sir?"

"Yes, please."

She left him with the cup of coffee and returned with a plate of eggs, potatoes, bacon, and bread. He took his time eating, savoring every bite.

She returned with more coffee.

"Where is the train station?" he asked.

"On the other side of the river and a few streets up," she replied. "There's a bridge across the river just north of the inn. Look for the engine smoke."

The blacksmith was putting coals in his furnace. He turned to Stepan. "Sleep well?"

"Yes."

"Follow me." He led Stepan to a small room at the back of the shop. "Here are your papers."

Stepan looked at the papers with the name Ivan Popov on them. "Ivan." He mouthed the name. "Now I am Ivan."

"You'll take a train to Milano."

"Italy?"

"I can only assume you're deserting and being followed. You don't want to go to Germany. Italy is safe. There are no *Okhrana* there. Do you speak Italian?"

"No."

"Most of the ticket agents and conductors speak German. Don't speak Yiddish except to the person you will meet in Milano."

Ivan nodded.

"You'll go to a boarding house at 23 Merlino Street. It's owned by Mrs. Belluno. Tell her you wish to rent a room for a week. If she says she has no room or when she asks for payment, show her the gold coin."

Ivan nodded.

"This is all I can do for you," said the blacksmith. "Good-bye."

"Thank you and good-bye." Ivan turned toward the door. This time he didn't look for Aza.

The walk to the station was short. The sun had begun its journey across the heavens. The city was coming to life. He heard the sound of a train. *My escape to Italy?* Excitement stirred within him.

Ivan entered the station. It was crowded. He found the ticket agent. "Milano, please."

"You'll have many stops and a four-hour delay in Zagreb to change trains. One way or round trip, sir?"

"One way, thank you."

"That will be thirty thousand leu, sir."

Ivan handed him some money saying, "I'm not familiar with your currency."

"Where're you from?"

Ivan hesitated. "East."

"I can be trusted," said the agent. He handed Ivan the change. "You can exchange your Romanian money here, but it will be better to exchange it in Milano because of your layover in Zagreb."

"Thank you. When does the train leave?"

The agent looked at his pocket watch. "In about an hour. There's a waiting room inside. I'll make sure you know when it's time to board."

"Thank you."

Ferka had told him it would be expensive. Ivan was grateful for his money. He didn't put all of it in his pocket, as Ferka had warned him to be careful. He put some in his satchel. The rest was tucked safely in his boot with his knife tucked in above it.

It didn't seem long before a train arrived. "You may board now, sir," said the agent. "The train will leave in twenty minutes."

Chapter 28

Ivan settled into a seat by the window. His mind drifted to Milano. He would be there in two and a half days.

He woke with a start. A baby cried for its breakfast. The car was bright with sunlight. Squinting, he looked out the window. The mountains were golden from the light of the sun. The sky was a brilliant blue. *What a beautiful day.*

He checked his watch—0900. His stomach growled. He found himself thinking about the wonderful meals he enjoyed at Ferka's. Reluctantly, he pulled a stale piece of pumpernickel bread from his satchel. *I wonder what Italian food will be like?*

Belgrade was a disappointment. He tried to purchase some food, but gave up. The language and currency were insurmountable obstacles.

He returned to the station. There were several new passengers waiting to board. He listened for Yiddish, but wasn't surprised when he heard none. Still, he was disappointed.

It was midafternoon on Monday when Ivan stepped off the train in Milano. He was amazed at the small size of the station. *I expected more. Surely, this isn't an indication of the size of the city.* He followed a group of passengers out of the station onto the street.

There Ivan stopped, his mouth open in amazement. The street was wide. There were buildings as far as he could see. The sidewalks were crowded with people and vendors. It was a bustling, noisy, moving collage of life. He felt excited. *Milano is quite different.* He stepped back into the station and approached the ticket master for directions to 23 Merlino Street.

In a short time, he arrived at the boardinghouse. It was attractive, white, three stories tall, and immaculate. He climbed the steps and knocked on the door. A short, stocky woman came to the door. She was wearing a long, blue dress with a white apron, her hands covered with flour, glasses looking like they would slide off her nose, and gray hair in a bun with strands sticking out in all directions.

Ivan held out his hand with the gold coin in his palm.

She opened the door and motioned him in. Ivan brushed passed her as she moved to the porch looking in all directions. "You're alone?" she asked in German.

Ivan nodded.

"I am Mrs. Belluno. I'll wash my hands and show you a room. Please take a seat and I'll be right back."

Ivan sat in a chair in the corner and studied the room. The space was bathed in brilliant light streaming through two long windows. A small chandelier glittered as light transformed its crystals into prisms of color on the walls. *Very pleasant.*

Mrs. Belluno returned. "Come, I'll show you the sleeping

quarters." She led Ivan up a wide stairway to the second floor and then up a narrow one to the third. The doorway to the room was at the top of the stairs. She stepped aside, allowing Ivan to enter. It was an impeccably clean room with a bed and matching dresser. A washstand was neatly tucked in the corner and a convenient chair sat by it. An oval mirror hung above the washstand.

"Very nice," said Ivan.

"There's a small bathroom," Mrs. Belluno said, pointing to a door. "This is the only room with a private bath. Let me see your papers."

Ivan pulled them from his satchel and gave them to her.

She examined the papers carefully. "You're the only refugee here at this time."

Refugee! I guess I am.

She handed back his papers. "My boarders will be here soon. Maybe it would be best if you stay in your room tonight. I will bring you some food before they arrive. We'll talk in the morning after they've gone. They leave by seven o'clock. Come down for breakfast after that. There will be no one here the rest of the day. I'm a Jew, but I'm also an Italian citizen. My reputation is as an Italian in the city and very few know I'm a Jew. It's important that I stay secure."

"I understand."

"I must finish supper."

Ivan nodded.

Mrs. Belluno disappeared down the stairs.

Ivan awoke to sunshine streaming in the window. He checked the time—0730. He washed, shaved, and combed his hair. *I wish I had clean clothes.* He went down the stairs. The house was quiet.

Mrs. Belluno greeted him with a smile as he entered the kitchen. "Now, aren't we the lazy one?"

Ivan blushed.

"Would you like some tea?"

"Yes, please."

Mrs. Belluno placed a plate of food before him. "Enjoy," she said with a broad smile.

"Thank you."

"I apologize for being so pushy yesterday. What I do is dangerous. I cannot be too careful."

Ivan nodded. *She's more fearful than Ferka's family was. Perhaps because she is alone.*

"These are hard times for us. I want to know nothing about you or your plans. This may seem harsh, but it's best for both of us. Let me tell you some things about the Jews here in Milano."

Ivan buttered a slice of dark bread.

"It's a different community than you might expect. The community is large and many are involved in the professions of law, finance, theater, and business. They have been very successful. However, a great many here are Jews in name only, not in practice.

She poured herself a cup of tea and offered him some more.

"No, thank you." He took a mouthful of food.

"They want to be Italian, recognized by the Italians, as Italians. They're highly identified with the Catholic Church. They have seen too much persecution—too much poverty. Do you understand?"

He shook his head while swallowing a bite of egg casserole.

"What you'll find is a rejection of the community if you don't identify yourself with Italy and the Catholics. I'm not saying you should or shouldn't do this. I'm only saying that this is what is happening here.

She stirred in a teaspoon of sugar, tasted her tea, and added a little more.

"Most coming here are not coming here for the freedom of being a Jew, but with the purpose of becoming Italians in every sense."

She took a sip of tea.

"My husband and I came here to escape the persecution in Russia, not to become Italians. I'm first a Jew and will remain so until my death. He passed away unexpectedly shortly after we bought this house."

"I'm sorry," said Ivan.

"I became a citizen and opened my home to boarders so I could survive and help others escape persecution. You, of course, can stay in the city as long as you want, but not here. I'll help you in any way I can. I've told you these things because I think it's important that you know what you're facing."

Ivan carried his empty plate to the sink.

"Thank you," she said.

Ivan nodded his understanding. "I appreciate what you have told me, Mrs. Belluno. I realize you're taking a risk in doing so.

"I've no fear of you. You could have taken that gold coin from another, but there's a mark on your papers that only someone who has helped you could have placed there."

"A mark?"

Mrs. Belluno didn't respond. She rose from the table, went to the sink, and began washing dishes.

I'm a man without a country. The reality of his position sank in. "I'll be leaving, Mrs. Belluno."

"Let me pack some food for you." She turned toward the stove. "I know you're probably going west or south. To go any other direction would be dangerous and foolish.

"Do you mean France?"

She nodded. "There's a Jewish community on the Atlantic coast—Saint Esprit—across the river from Bayonne. It's not the only Jewish community in France, but it's the largest and is known to be a secure community."

"Saint Esprit?"

She nodded. "There's much employment on ships and access to many countries where it's safer for Jews—including America."

She handed Ivan a package.

"This will be enough for your journey. There are no guarantees in this dangerous world. The coin is your passport out of Europe."

"Thank you. May I pay you?"

"No."

Ivan nodded. "I don't speak French."

"Your German will serve you well on the train. Once you are in Saint Esprit, you can safely speak Yiddish. Good-bye and God speed."

Ivan turned and walked out the front door.

At the train station, he bought a one-way ticket to Saint Esprit. The seat by the window gave him a nice view of the country. The *Okhrana* office in Paris weighed on his mind. *Will I ever be safe?*

Chapter 29

Ivan arrived in Saint Esprit by midafternoon the next day. He approached the ticket agent and asked in Yiddish, "I understand this to be a Jewish community. Is this correct?"

"There are many Jews here, if that is what you mean. Perhaps I can help you. Are you looking for a particular person or place?"

"Can you direct me to a boardinghouse and a cafe?"

"Yes, there are two boardinghouses on *Vue Sur le Fleuve*. Go from the station and turn right. Go one kilometer and turn left. The first one will be on your right—the fourth house. The second will be one-half kilometer further on the left. You'll pass several eating establishments along the way."

"And where can I exchange currency?

"There is a bank a short distance up the road on your left."

"Thank you," said Ivan.

He had no trouble finding a building that looked like a bank, but he wasn't sure. As he stood looking at the building, a young man approached him.

"*Bonjour*."

Ivan looked at him with a blank look on his face. He held up the palms of his hands and shrugged. "I don't understand," he said in German.

This time the young man looked at Ivan with a blank look

and held his palms up. They both laughed.

"Is this the bank?" Ivan asked in Yiddish.

"Yes, it is," replied the man in the same language.

"Thank you."

The man nodded and continued on his way.

How nice to be able to speak openly.

Ivan went into the bank, exchanged his Italian lire for French francs, and continued his journey toward the boardinghouse. In a short distance, he noticed a building with a sign over the door displaying a plate of food. His stomach growled. *I'm starving!* He entered and surveyed the room. Two men at a table in the corner were laughing. "That's funny," said one in Yiddish.

Ivan walked to the table. "Excuse me, my name is Ivan. I just arrived in Saint Esprit and I know no one here. May I join you?"

The two men looked at him for a moment and then one spoke, "My name is Jacob. This is my brother Aaron." They both stood and shook hands with Ivan. "Please sit," said Jacob, motioning to a chair.

"Thank you. You are kind."

A server appeared with two plates of food and set them before the two brothers. Looking at Ivan, she said, "May I get you something to eat, sir?"

Ivan looked at the food with a puzzled face. "What is this?" he asked, pointing toward a plate.

Aaron laughed. "It's a cheese soufflé. It's very good."

"I believe you'd enjoy it, sir," said the server.

Ivan nodded.

"Would you like something to drink, sir?"

"Yes, water and coffee."

After the server walked away, Ivan whispered, "What is a cheese soufflé?"

Jacob chuckled. "It is a light, fluffy baked dish made with egg yolks and beaten egg whites. Soufflé means to blow up, but obviously it isn't blown up so we say puffed up. These two are made with Parmesan cheese, crabmeat, corn, onions and spices. Soufflé's also make a wonderful dessert when mixed with chocolate, powdered sugar, and other sweets."

"Stop," said Ivan. "My stomach is growling." Ivan put both hands on his stomach.

"Perhaps you'll want more than one," said Jacob with a laugh.

"You may be right. Please, eat. Don't wait for me."

The men didn't hesitate.

"You're not familiar with the French. Where do you come from?"

"Italy." *I did come from Milano.*

"What brings you to Saint Esprit?" asked Aaron.

"I'm looking for work," said Ivan, not willing to say more.

"There's much work here," said Jacob.

The waitress returned with a glass of water and a steaming cup of coffee. She set both in front of Ivan.

"Thank you." Ivan took a long drink of water.

"Where are you going now, Ivan?" asked Aaron.

"To a boardinghouse on *Vue Sur le Fleuve*."

Both men laughed heartily. "That was quite a pronunciation," said Aaron. "I hope you didn't say it that way to a Frenchman."

Ivan blushed. He stirred in some cream and a spoon of sugar into his coffee. He took a sip and nodded his approval.

"Don't worry, you'll catch on. We're going in the direction of your boardinghouse," said Jacob. "You can walk with us. We'll make sure you get there. A Frenchman might take you to another address just to be devious." The brothers laughed again. This time Ivan laughed with them.

"It's a short walk, maybe twenty minutes," said Jacob.

"Thank you, I'll enjoy the walk. I've been on the train for some time, and it feels good to stretch my legs."

The server brought his food. "Enjoy, sir."

"Thank you."

Ivan sampled a bite, smiled, and nodded. He had to restrain himself from gobbling it down.

"Saint Esprit is a beautiful city," said Ivan. "I understand it's a Jewish community." He took another sip of coffee.

"Not entirely," replied Aaron, "but mostly. The work on the ships has attracted many. We are hard workers. The ship owners appreciate that."

"There is no persecution here," said Jacob. "Many of us own businesses. Some are ship officers. It is a good life. Aaron and I are carpenters. We build and repair homes and businesses. We built this establishment."

Ivan looked around the room with a more critical eye. "Very nice. You do good work."

"Thank you," said Aaron.

Jacob nodded.

"That was wonderful," said Ivan, rubbing his stomach.

"Can you eat another?" asked Jacob.

"Probably, but I'm tired and need to sleep." Ivan stretched. "I'll finish my coffee and refrain from indulging more."

The three men walked out of the restaurant to a beautiful setting sun. It was a fast walk to the boardinghouse. They made plans to meet at six o'clock for breakfast. The brothers bid Ivan goodnight.

The next morning, Ivan found Jacob and Aaron already seated at a table with mugs of hot coffee. A third man sat with them. He had a black beard that covered a tanned leathery face; Ivan thought he wasn't much older than thirty.

"Ah, good morning, Ivan. You slept well?" asked Aaron.

"Yes, my bed was quite comfortable."

"Good. This is our friend Joseph," said Jacob. "Joseph, meet our new friend, Ivan."

"Ah, the pleasure is mine," said Joseph with a heavy French accent. He stood and extended his hand to Ivan.

"Likewise," Ivan replied as he took Joseph's hand. It was a firm handshake. *He must be six inches taller and fifty pounds heavier than me.* Ivan sat down at the table. Jacob handed him a menu. Ivan ordered coffee, bagels, and lox.

"You are, how you say, a newcomer?" asked Joseph.

"Yes, I just arrived yesterday."

"From where did you come?"

"Italy," replied Ivan.

"And for what?"

Ivan hesitated.

"I mean, for what did you come to Saint Esprit?"

"I'm looking for work."

The waitress brought Ivan's breakfast. He thanked her and took a sip of coffee.

"Have you seen the Atlantic?" asked Joseph.

"No, but I'm looking forward to seeing it. Is Bayonne a large port?" asked Ivan.

"So so," shrugged Joseph.

"Large enough to be very busy," replied Aaron. "There are numerous ships going to countless ports, including America."

America!

"You said yesterday that you want employment. What is your experience?" asked Aaron.

Ivan thought for a moment. He took another sip of coffee. *What is my experience?* "I've been a farm laborer and a hunter," replied Ivan.

"Neither of those types of work exists in Saint Esprit, but being a farm laborer means you're used to hard work" said Jacob.

Ivan nodded, remembering how sore his hands were at Ferka's.

"I work on a ship," said Joseph. "It is steady and it pays well."

"Do you go to sea?" asked Ivan.

"Yes, I love the water. I live on a ship and never miss the land."

"Joseph has no special lady in his life," said Aaron laughing. "That's why he stays at sea so long."

"This is true! I just have not met the right woman to tame me," said Joseph with a broad grin.

"Many have tried, though," said Jacob. "Besides, he loves the ladies in all the ports, don't you, Joseph?"

"I cannot resist. Perhaps all the ladies, in all the ports." Joseph threw his head back laughing.

Ivan looked at the brothers. Aaron shrugged and Jacob shook his head.

"Perhaps there is a lady in your life, Ivan?" said Joseph.

Rachael! Ivan cleared his throat and took a drink of coffee. "No."

"There are many to choose from here. No arranged marriages in this community," said Aaron. "We can introduce you to as many as you like."

"Ooh la la! Do not let them talk you into anything, *mon ami*," said Joseph with a wink.

"What does that mean?"

Joseph gave Ivan a curious look. "It means, don't let them talk you into marriage."

"No, I mean *mon ami*."

Joseph let out a loud laugh. "It means my friend. You don't speak French?"

"No. I won't."

Joseph looked puzzled. "You won't speak French?"

Ivan blushed. "No, I mean I won't let them talk me into marriage. Right now I need to find work."

"Ah! I think we have frustrated the young man," Joseph said with another loud laugh.

"We can always use a hard worker. Are you interested?" asked Jacob.

Ivan was grateful to Jacob for rescuing him. "This is very generous of you and much more than I hoped for. However, the thought of working on a ship intrigues me."

"Ah! Wanderlust! She has captured you?" asked Joseph stroking his beard.

"Perhaps."

Joseph pounded his fist on the table. "I think you will make a fine sailor. I will be happy to show you the port, *mon ami*," said Joseph. "In fact, I insist. I am headed that way. It is only five kilometers to the port. My ship leaves in two days for Spain."

"I've never been to Spain."

"Well, then, you have something to look forward to . . . that is if you really want to go to sea and if the captain will hire you."

"I think I would like to go to sea," said Ivan.

"Good! It is settled. The ocean has more scents than a woman," said Joseph. "You'll experience all of them and more. Come, let us go see if the sea is calling you as it calls me."

"Can I pay for your breakfasts?" Ivan asked the men.

"Absolutely not!" exclaimed Jacob. "You're our guest.

Once you find employment then we'll let you buy . . . all the time."

"Ah, but you may pay for mine," said Joseph.

All four laughed.

"Then this is good-bye for now," said Ivan.

"Good luck to you," said Jacob. "May God grant you much success in all you do."

Ivan walked to the port with Joseph. The sun was a golden globe set in the darkest blue sky Ivan had ever seen. There wasn't a cloud in the heavens. A gentle breeze blew in from the coast. Birds were everywhere.

"Is the weather always this pleasant?" asked Ivan.

"But of course. You see how the flowers grow? They are as beautiful as the women. If I were a landlubber, this is where I would live, mon ami. It is near perfect."

Ivan stooped down and picked a flower. Putting it to his nose, he breathed in the aroma.

"Were you born in Saint Esprit?"

"No, Paris."

Paris.

"You moved to Saint Esprit for work?"

"No, Paris is too big. Too noisy. You cannot breathe there. There is a river that comes from the Atlantic, but it is not the same as living on the sea. Ships have to dock at the ports of Rouen or LeHavre and cargoes have to be transported from there."

"I see. It appears to be very prosperous here. The buildings are well taken care of."

"But, of course, *mon ami*. We French are very proud."

A man walked toward them, tipping his hat as they passed.

"Good morning," he said.

"Good morning to you," replied Ivan.

Everyone is so friendly. I like this freedom. He smiled to himself and quickened his pace.

"You are in a hurry?" called Joseph.

Ivan laughed. "I guess I am." He slowed down. As they topped a rise, the port came into view.

The sun lit up the azure water as far as the eye could see. At least a dozen ships sat at anchor in the harbor and more caressed the docks. Two were steaming toward the open sea leaving a trail of dark smoke. Ivan stopped to take in the entire scene. "This is beautiful," he whispered. The smell of fish curled up his nostrils. There were wagons everywhere and men were swarming like ants, carrying boxes and sacks.

Joseph's voice broke Ivan's trance. "It is a stunning sight, is it not?"

"Yes, it is," replied Ivan. "It's like a painting."

"Yes, even when it's raining and windy, it is a gorgeous sight. I never tire of it."

"I hope I can find work. I know what you mean about the sea calling you. She is like a lady."

"I am quite confident you will find work on my ship. If, by chance, the Captain is not hiring, you can go to another. They are always coming and going. I have never seen a man have to wait more than a few hours to find work."

This is very good.

"Which is your ship, Joseph?"

"The *Reine de la Mer*. Do you see that row of five ships? She is the one in the middle and a fine vessel she is. Come with me to meet Captain Reuben."

They headed down the hill to the row of ships with Joseph chatting about the ships and the sea—his hands and arms waving like tree limbs in the wind.

"Here we are, Ivan. My ship, my life."

Ivan stood looking at the ship in awe. "It's very large."

In the distance a bell rang three times. "It's 0730," said Joseph. "Time for me to get aboard."

Ivan followed Joseph up the gangway. As they stepped onto the ship, a large, muscular man looked up from a table. His beard was long and thick—more gray than black. A black stocking cap sat on the back of his head.

"Ah, Joseph, you old rascal." The words rolled out around his pipe. Smoke puffed out of the pipe and his mouth.

"Good morning, Captain."

"Who is this with you?"

"My friend, Ivan, who is looking for work."

"Greetings, Ivan," said the Captain, extending his hand.

"Greetings, Captain Reuben," Ivan took his hand.

"The men just call me Captain. What's your experience?" he asked, the pipe clenched in his teeth.

"I have no experience on a ship, but I work hard. I've been a farm laborer."

"Hmm. This isn't a farm," he laughed. "You must be a

hard worker to live on my ship. Let me think. What would be like farm work? We have no fields to plow. No cows to milk. No goats to feed. No sheep." His humor was contagious and all three men laughed heartily. Then there was silence. "But you are serious, aren't you?" asked the Captain staring Ivan in his eyes.

"Yes sir, I'm very serious."

"We're loading for Spain this trip. They love the Bayonne chocolates in Barcelona so we must take them a supply. We start filling my ship today. I'll work you hard. We'll see how you do on the first voyage."

"Thank you, sir. I'm looking forward to it."

"Then welcome aboard. Joseph will give you a tour of the ship. After that, you'll find out what it's really like to work."

Ivan followed Joseph through a hatchway to the interior of the ship.

"That is the hatch. Do not make the mistake of calling it the door. The men will have no mercy on you if you do."

Ivan frowned.

"Do not worry, *mon ami*, you will learn fast. Your ears are your best friends. My suggestion is that you do not talk much—listen. The Captain does not like talking when we are loading and unloading. He wants the work done. While we are underway, there is an abundance of time for conversation. We have a good crew. You will like most them. There will always be one or two who will twist you in knots."

"Twist me in knots?"

"Ah, you will understand. The wind, she is always twisting

rope in knots. She does not let up."

Ivan looked up at the rigging. There was constant movement as the wind blew through. He nodded at Joseph and determined to follow his advice.

"I will now show you the hold where the cargo is stored," said Joseph. "You will probably be working down there most of the time. It is hot and dim. You will most certainly work up a sweat and go through some testing. They will want to see if you are a man or if you just look like one."

Ivan nodded. He rubbed his palms on his pants.

"Follow me down the ladder. Watch your step and grip tightly. You do not want to fall. The rungs are usually wet and slippery. I will not go slow as I am one of the crew. You are sure to get much harassment, as they will be quick to recognize you are a new man. Joke back to them. It will be easier for you. If they think you cannot take it, they will increase the torment. This will be your initiation."

Ivan swallowed hard and nodded.

Halfway down, one of the men below started laughing and jeering. "What do we have here? A landlubber?"

"Yah! Look how he is hugging the ladder," shouted another. "And so slow. It must be a girl."

There was much laughter.

"This is Ivan," said Joseph when they reached the deck. "He has never been on a ship before. He is not only a landlubber, he is a farmer. The Captain will have him butchering cows tomorrow."

The men roared.

"Did you think there'd be cows to milk down here?" heckled another. "Maybe you'd like to plant some pretty flowers,"

They looked at Ivan expectantly.

"I was hoping I'd get to gather eggs from the chickens," Ivan quipped.

There was a burst of laughter.

"Enough!"

Ivan recognized the Russian accent.

"Get back to work," barked a giant of a man pushing through. A jagged scar ran from his left ear to his chin. "We have work to do. Get to it." He pointed to Ivan. "Do not disrupt my men again."

Ivan felt the eyes of every man on him to see how he would respond.

Ivan turned toward Joseph.

Joseph jerked his head toward the ladder.

At the top of the ladder, Ivan said, "I've never seen a man that big. He's taller than you and outweighs you by a good twenty-five kilograms. Why is his face so disfigured?"

"I don't know. He's been on the ship less than a month. He doesn't talk about it and I doubt anyone has the nerve to ask him. You can if you want to."

"I don't think so," Stepan replied as the two men returned to the Captain.

"How did he do, Joseph?" asked the Captain.

"He did fine, Captain. The men gave him the usual

welcome."

"Ha! They bite hard sometimes, but they're a good bunch. It's a tradition. You'll get to know them individually."

Ivan nodded.

"Now, let me see if I've something for a farm laborer to do. How much can you carry?"

"I don't know. I've never calculated."

"You'll know soon enough."

The Captain winked at Joseph.

"Go back to the hold and find the Giant. You know who I mean?"

"Yes," Ivan swallowed.

"He's your boss."

"Stack those boxes on the port side," said the Giant pointing to the right side of the cargo bay.

After Ivan stacked the boxes for an hour, the Giant said, "I said the port side. Didn't you hear me?"

"Yes, I stacked them where you pointed."

"You think I don't know port from starboard!" shouted the man. "Everyone knows the difference between port and starboard. Why would I point to the right side when port means left? Stack those boxes where they belong. You better get smart, sailor, and fast."

Chapter 30

"This is the mess, *mon ami*," said Joseph. "It is where we satisfy our belly. You will be spending a lot of time in here when we're at sea. It is the social gathering place. Coffee is always available and any leftover foods."

"Mess, ladders, decks, hatches, rails, portals, port, starboard . . . the sea certainly has its own language," said Ivan.

"It does indeed. You are just getting started, but you are a quick learner. Are you ready for some chow?"

Ivan determined Joseph meant food. "I could eat a cow. I've never worked this hard."

Joseph laughed. "You are a farmer, undeniably. Grab a plate, tray, and some silver, and go through that line. No matter how much they throw on your plate, you must eat it all. Another ritual."

Ivan held out his plate while the servers piled on the chow.

"I'll weigh a ton after I eat this meal."

"You may and you will have a harder time this afternoon being as full as you will be. The Giant will be watching you to see how you hold up. He wants to know if he can break you down. Do not allow him to do it."

"I'm determined," said Ivan. "I have seen his kind before. What's his name?"

"I've never heard him called anything else."

"Go to the fantail and bring back a box of bulkheads," commanded the Giant.

What's the fantail? I'm not going to ask him.

"The fantail is at the front of the ship," said a sailor polishing a brass bell.

"You've come to the wrong place," said another, using a wire brush to scrape rust from an anchor chain. "The fantail is where the steering wheel is."

On the bridge, he was sent to the galley. When he got to the galley, he met the cooks and found out that the fantail was at the very rear of the ship, which is aft. There he found a box labeled bulkheads nailed shut.

"Here are the bulkheads," he said to the Giant.

"He found the bulkheads," shouted the Gant. "It took you long enough to find a simple place." The laughter echoed around the hold.

"Take off the lid."

Ivan found a bar and pried off the lid. There was a length of chain.

"Apparently, he doesn't know the difference between a chain and a bulkhead," roared the Giant. "Someone show him what a bulkhead is."

One of the men slapped a wall. "This is a bulkhead, landlubber. Every sailor knows this."

Ivan stood in the shower laughing at himself. The water

felt good. He'd been told to take a short shower. "There's water as far as the eye can see, but fresh water is precious on a ship."

He took his time drying off and went to his bunk.

Joseph stuck his head in the compartment Ivan shared with fifteen others.

"You alone, *mon ami*?"

"For the moment, they're giving me a rest from the harassment."

"Ah, the Giant, he worked you over?"

"More than that," Ivan said, rubbing his back.

"But, how did you handle it?"

"Whatever he said, I did." Ivan stretched his back. "I know where the fantail, bow, bridge, galley, and head are."

"Ha! You are starting to sound like a sailor."

"I'd rather read a book about ships."

Joseph laughed.

"You will have three watches to get over it."

"That's a new term. What's a watch?" Ivan started brushing his hair.

"Each day is broken into three shifts—the day, evening, and midnight. Each shift is called a watch. You will start with an evening watch, then the day watch, and finish with the midnight watch. Then you are off seven watches. The only time this routine is broken is if the sea is angry with us. She will try to bury us in her depths. Then we must secure everything and batten down the ship. She will toss us around like a toy."

Ivan shook his head. "Sounds dangerous."

"It is, mon ami, you have seen nothing like it."

"Why do I have three watches off after working only eight hours? I thought you said three shifts."

"I did, but the first day is different. It is the Captain's way. The first watch allows him to see how hard you work and how you interact with the men. He then gives you three watches to work out some of the soreness and find your way around the ship. It will also give you time to get used to the movement of the ship."

"I've had no trouble so far."

"Ah, but you will. We will be able to see how you are doing by your color."

"My color?"

"Yes. If you are having trouble, you will turn green."

"That doesn't sound so good."

"You will, of course, survive." Joseph said with a smile. "We have already placed wagers on you."

"Wagers? On me?"

"But of course, *mon ami*. It is tradition."

"Did you bet I will turn green?"

Joseph just smiled.

Ivan let out a heavy sigh. "Will I continue to work for the Giant?"

"But, of course. It is the Captain's wish."

Ivan groaned. "I'm going to dream about him."

"Ha! That will be a nightmare. I am on the mid watch and should get some sleep, but since this is our last night in port, most of us are going ashore for a farewell toast to Bayonne. It is a tradition. You will come?"

Ivan hesitated. "Yes, I think if I'm going to be a sailor, I should be one in every respect."

"Good," said Joseph. "I'm going to change my clothes. You are already to go?"

"I'll be topside when you're ready."

"See, you are learning the language already, *mon ami*."

Ivan smiled to himself. Yes, I am.

The sun looked like a huge orange dipping into the sea, the water was like glass, and a light breeze was blowing off the ocean. *I think I'll really enjoy being a sailor.* He thought over the schedule and settled it firm in his mind. He looked past the ships to the sea. The water stretched as far as he could see until the water merged with the sky. *There's so much to see of this world. What's beyond? It'll be worth whatever price I have to pay.*

"Here I am," said Joseph. We should eat before we go."

"More food?" Ivan made a face.

"They will not be as hard on you this evening. You can tell them how much you want from now on. You have earned enough respect to do so."

"How do you know this?" Ivan raised his eyebrows.

"The word, it travels fast on this ship. The Giant harassed you much today and you took it well."

They went through the line and Ivan picked out what food he wanted and indicated the amount of each. He saw many smiles.

Walking off the mess deck, Joseph said, "It is a perfect evening. Have you had any French wine?"

"No, I don't drink."

"Surely you jest! It is the best in the world. It goes down like velvet and primes you for more. Wine is a common drink in French homes. I do like it, but I have seen what it can do. I would prefer not to let myself get in that condition, especially when we are going to sea tomorrow. There is no sense in complicating matters if we encounter an angry woman out there. Besides, the Captain does not tolerate less than the best form."

Ivan nodded his understanding.

"Then, let us go ashore. Some of the men may already be there."

They walked along the shore toward the city.

"This port is fascinating," said Ivan. "Is each ship the same?"

"Not at all, *mon ami*. Each crew comes from countries all over the world, the cargoes are different, and each ship has its own destination."

"So, there are specific routes?"

"No, it may be a long time before we get back to Bayonne. We do not normally know where we are going. It is from one port to the next. It is entirely up to the Captain."

Ivan scratched his head. "What about families?"

"Ah, very few of the men have families. Those who work at loading or unloading cargoes live here. The rest of us go to sea to man the ship and keep her safe. The Captain hires those he needs in ports to unload and load cargo."

"How long have you been on board?"

"Four years with the Captain, but there have been other ships."

"How many?" asked Ivan.

Joseph counted on his fingers. "Six. The first one was when I was eighteen, fourteen years ago."

"You have been at sea a long time." said Ivan. "What do you do?"

"I am the quartermaster. I determine the course for the Captain based on the sun, moon, and stars."

"How do you do that? You must have exceptionally good eyes."

"Ah, it is more complicated than that. I will show you when we set sail. You have much to learn."

"I'm sure you're right. But, our ship doesn't have sails."

"Ha! It's a figure of speech from the days when all ships had sails."

Chapter 31

"Here we are, *mon ami*," said Joseph stopping in front of an old building.

Ivan heard music and laughter coming from inside. "It sounds like they have started without us," he said.

"Let us go in and add to the festivities," said Joseph, his eyes twinkling.

They entered the cabaret and stopped to adjust their eyes to the dimness. It was crowded, noisy, and filled with a mixture of smells—ale, burning tobacco, lamp oil, sawdust, dirt, and food. The walls were of rough lumber and the floor was dirt covered with a thick layer of sawdust. The conversation was loud. Shouting and laughter filled the air.

Several men waved as they saw Joseph and motioned him to come to their table. Ivan recognized some of them. The Giant was not among them. Ivan was relieved.

"The ship is well represented," said Joseph with a laugh, as they walked toward the others. "To you who do not know him, this is my friend Ivan," said Joseph. He slapped Ivan on his back.

They all shook Ivan's hand and welcomed him.

A beautiful young French girl came up to them. Ivan enjoyed Joseph's response. Although he didn't understand what Joseph said, he felt confident the older man was flirting. The girl seemed to enjoy it. Ivan enjoyed the sound of the language. *This is beginning to feel like home.*

They sat down with four others. The conversation was continuous and the laughter was hearty.

This reminds me of the camp days with Nikolai.

"Ivan!" It was Pierre, a man who worked in the boiler room. "Would you be my partner?"

"What game are you playing? I'm not good with cards."

"No, no. This is a man's game." He pointed to a target on the wall.

"Ah, knife throwing."

"You're familiar with the game?" asked Pierre?

Ivan nodded, "I used to throw hunting knives in my village." *I better be careful about what I say.*

The waitress interrupted, requesting their drink order.

"No thank you," replied Joseph, "we're leaving for Paris in the morning and I'm on duty at midnight."

"Paris! I thought we were going to Spain."

"We were, *mon ami*, but things have changed. The Captain told me to chart the course to Paris yesterday. Why are you frowning? We will be there for a whole week. There are many mademoiselles waiting for us.

Ivan nodded.

"Are you good at knife throwing, Pierre?" asked Ivan.

"Sometime yes, sometimes no. I don't know yet tonight. Are you?"

"Possibly we're the same." Ivan smiled.

"It's only a game, but there is usually some currency involved."

Ivan hesitated. "I have little money."

"Don't worry, it's not much, only a small amount to make it interesting."

"Go ahead, *mon ami*" said Joseph. "I will advance you some francs. If you lose, you do not have to pay me until the Captain pays you."

"All right, I'll play."

"There's a game in progress," said Pierre. "I'll signal we want to challenge the winners." He placed a coin on a table near the target. One of the men playing nodded.

"What are the rules?" asked Ivan.

"Are you familiar with horseshoes?"

"Yes," said Ivan.

"The winners throw first. A knife in the bull's-eye and you score three points. The next ring is two . . . the next, one. The game goes to twenty-one and you must win by two points."

Ivan nodded. "You keep playing until someone wins by two?"

"Yes. Sometimes a game can last a while if the players are equally matched. There are several knives to choose from."

"Can I use my own knife?"

Pierre hesitated. "Perhaps, if the other three players agree, but it may not be such a good idea. Some take the game more seriously than others."

"I understand. It's only a game," he said, dismissing the idea.

"Are you ready? We're up next," said Pierre.

Ivan watched the game in process with interest. The players harassed each man as he threw. Some had been drinking for a while and had trouble hitting the target. People walking past the game gave them a wide space in case a knife ricocheted off the wall. No one wanted to lose an eye or end up under a doctor's needle.

Soon it was Ivan and Pierre's turn to play.

The first man barely missed the bull's-eye. Pierre looked at Ivan and raised his eyebrows.

"You first," said Ivan.

Pierre threw wide. "This may be a bad night." He smiled sheepishly.

The next opponent hit the bull's-eye.

"I see why you won the last game," said Ivan to the man.

The man grunted.

Ivan's throw stuck in the outer ring.

"Five to two," said one of the opponents smiling.

"It's just the start," said Ivan. He warmed up, but Pierre didn't. They lost.

"Looks like we'll be sitting out for a while," said Pierre.

Ivan put a coin on the table and looked around for Joseph. He was sitting with a beautiful woman. He looked at Ivan and winked. *Reminds me of Nikolai's wink.* Ivan winked back.

Two games passed before they could play again. The room seemed to get noisier as the night wore on.

"Our turn again, Ivan. I'll follow you this time."

The first opponent threw a point.

Ivan balanced his knife, studied the target, fixed his eye, and threw.

"Bull's-eye!" shouted Pierre.

They won two games in a row.

Ivan checked his watch. *2300.*

"That's a nice pocket watch you have," said a man with a Russian accent. "May I see it?"

Ivan's blood turned cold. He held the watch out for the man to see, but didn't let him take it. *How could I be so stupid! This man could be Okhrana. Vasile knows this watch. He would have given them a description.*

"Would you be interested in selling it to me?"

"No," said Ivan.

"Pity. I'd like to add it to my collection."

Ivan ignored the comment.

Joseph slapped Ivan on the back. "Good throwing, *mon ami*. We should leave now. It is better to get back early than late. The Captain is not tolerant of lateness and has been known to shorten a man's pay."

Ivan said good night to Pierre. The two shook hands.

"I'm going to say good-night to my lady friend," said Joseph. "She needs at least one more kiss to remember me by."

"I'll meet you outside," said Ivan.

He stepped outside and walked toward the edge of the building. Two men stepped out of the shadows.

Ivan recognized the Russian. He didn't know the other.

"Show me that watch," demanded the Russian.

The second man circled around behind Ivan.

Ivan turned with his back to the cabaret wall.

"There's no need. I'm not selling it."

"Then, I will have to take it from you."

Ivan lunged at the Russian, catching him off guard, and threw him to the ground. The second man started toward him.

Joseph stepped out of the building. Seeing what was going on, he grabbed the man from behind and sent him flying face-first to the ground. The man didn't move.

Ivan had pinned his man facedown. He pulled the Russian's head up by his hair, pulled his knife from his boot, and slipped it under the Russian's chin. He asked in a husky whisper, "Who are you?"

"I'm only interested in your watch."

"I don't think so," said Ivan, pulling the man's hair tighter.

"It's Russian. It reminds me of home. I had one just like it," he wheezed.

"I think not. Why would you approach me in this manner? The truth!"

There was no answer. Ivan pulled back tighter moving the knife closer to his neck. "You're *Okhrana*?"

Again no answer. Ivan pulled the man's hair even tighter and pressed the knife against his throat. A trickle of blood dripped to the ground.

"Yes!" he squeaked.

At that moment, some of the men from the ship came out of the cabaret. *Thank God we're leaving port in the morning*. He let the Russian go and slipped his knife back into his boot. Ivan got up and looked around. He saw the other man lying facedown. He looked at Joseph and nodded his appreciation.

"What happened?" asked Pierre.

"It's just a misunderstanding, isn't it?" Ivan asked the Russian who'd gotten up.

"Yes, a misunderstanding," the Russian said with his hand covering his throat.

"You'll need to attend to your friend," said Ivan to the Russian. "It appears he may need help."

The Russian glared at Ivan without saying anything.

Ivan turned and started walking, Joseph beside him. They walked in silence while Pierre and the rest of the men followed them whispering. *There will be questions tomorrow. I'll have to think carefully how I'm going to answer them.*

"You did well, Joseph. Thank you for helping me."

"It was nothing, *mon ami*. All I did was trip him. It happened very fast. What were you saying to the Russian? I could not hear you."

"I just wanted to know why my watch was of such importance to him."

"This was all over a watch? What did he say?"

"In the cabaret, he said he collected watches and wanted to buy mine. I told him no. I guess he doesn't take no for an answer."

"This is interesting," replied Joseph. "He must have had too much to drink. Why else would he have tried to take it from you when you said no?"

"Who can understand people?" shrugged Ivan.

When they boarded the ship, Joseph went to the quartermaster's room for duty. Ivan went below. He climbed onto his bunk in his clothes. As hard as he tried, it was useless—he could not sleep. Thoughts of the *Okhrana* filled his mind. *How did they find me? How did they track me to Saint Esprit?*

He jumped out of his bunk and went topside, hoping he could escape his thoughts. The cool breeze off the ocean blew through his hair as if trying to purge his mind. A parade of faces passed through—Momma, Israel, Rachael, Ferka. *Are they safe? The Okhrana couldn't know I was in Saint Esprit.* Suddenly a grotesque image of Vasile was staring at him. *Vasile has told them everything about me . . . Nikolai's pocket watch, my knife . . . everything. I should have known. How foolish of me! At least I'm safe on this ship, but if they get word to Paris before we get there, they'll be waiting for me.*

He let the sound of the ocean hypnotize him until the sky turned gray followed by hints of gold as the sun began making its appearance.

Chapter 32

Ivan watched Joseph as he strolled across the mess deck toward him.

"Good morning, *mon ami*," said Joseph as he sat down at the table. "You're up early."

"I've been awake all night."

"Too much excitement last night I think."

Ivan nodded. "I may be able to sleep now."

"Not this morning, *mon ami*. We are about to get underway. You do not want to miss leaving the port. I have been on watch all night so you are no more tired than I and I only have eight hours off."

"Why? You were on the mid watch so you should be off three watches."

"Not so, mon ami. When we are going to sea, I have one watch on and one off until we have been underway a day. I must set us on the course and complete the charts for Captain."

Pierre waved as he came through the hatch. He joined them at the table. "How's the champion knife thrower?" Pierre asked.

"Hardly a champion," replied Ivan. "I was lucky."

"Hmm, I don't think so lucky. Maybe I'd think so if I hadn't seen you use it on that Russian."

"What's for breakfast?" asked Ivan ignoring the comment. He could feel Joseph's stare as he went through the chow line. The cooks and servers didn't ask any questions, but Ivan could tell there was a difference in their respect. Several acknowledged him with a nod, placed the food on his tray gently rather than slopping it, and waited to see if he wanted more.

At ten o'clock, the ship left port. Ivan and Joseph stood on the fantail, watching the deck hands casting off the lines that held the ship to the pier.

"This is my favorite place when we ship out," said Joseph. "Every man has his place. It's like a ritual."

"There are a lot of customs," commented Ivan.

"Yes, I told you the sea is like a woman. She caresses us with her waves. We never know if she is going to be gentle or throw us around in a rage. I have seen her smooth as silk, without a ripple, and I have seen her waves fifteen meters high."

"Fifteen meters!" exclaimed Ivan.

"*Oui*, we have taken a forty degree roll in her rage."

Ivan held out his arm trying to imagine a forty degree roll.

"The curtains on the mess deck stood nearly straight out. I did not think she was going to let the ship come back upright."

"Were you afraid?" Ivan questioned.

"Everyone on board was afraid."

"And you still go to sea?"

"Ah, but yes, and I always will. It is never the same out

there. There is no land in sight. Occasionally we see another ship, but for the most part, we are all alone. There is a peace to it that cannot be explained. You will know what I mean after this voyage."

It was silent as the two friends watched Bayonne grow smaller and smaller until it disappeared.

"I better get some sleep," said Joseph. "Wake me for supper?"

"Certainly."

Ivan leaned on the rail staring at the wake behind the ship. A great sadness suddenly overtook him. He watched as the continent slipped away. The uncertainty about his family haunted him. *What of the men from the Okhrana? Do they know I'm on this ship?*

"Ivan."

Startled from his thoughts, Ivan turned toward the voice.

"The Captain wants to see you in his quarters," said a server from the chow line.

Ivan started to ask why, but the man turned away and disappeared through a hatch.

As Ivan stepped away from the rail, the ship rolled slightly causing him to lurch toward the bulkhead. *My stomach feels funny.* Then the ship rolled slightly in the other direction causing him to step toward the rail. He reached out to stop himself and stood still for a minute until he was stable. He looked to see if anyone was watching—no one. He took a deep breath and headed toward the Captain's compartment.

Ivan knocked on the Captain's door.

"Enter."

He removed his cap as he entered. "You wanted to see me, Captain?"

"Sit down, Ivan. Would you like some coffee?"

"No, sir, thank you."

The Captain poured a cup for himself and sat down across from Ivan. He crossed his legs, took a sip from the cup, and said, "I understand you were in a scuffle last night. Were you hurt?"

"No, sir."

The Captain took another swallow of coffee while studying Ivan.

"How did it happen?"

"A Russian liked my pocket watch and wanted me to sell it to him. I refused."

"May I see the watch?" The Captain held out his hand.

Ivan detached the gold chain from his belt loop and handed the watch to the Captain.

"It's a beautiful watch. It is unusual with this gold pick attached. I can understand you not wanting to sell it. Did it belong to your father?"

"No. I inherited it when a close friend passed away."

"I see." The Captain handed the watch back to Ivan. "The fight occurred outside the tavern?"

"Yes." Ivan smoothed back his hair.

"Had you been drinking?"

"No sir, I don't drink," said Ivan. He shifted in his chair.

"Are you nervous?" asked the Captain, raising his eyebrows.

"A little."

"You were with Joseph, weren't you?" The Captain smiled.

"Yes, sir."

"He's a good man. I understand there were two men. Is this true?"

"Yes. They had me cornered when Joseph came out. He knocked one to the ground."

"I'm told you handled yourself very well. Where did you learn to fight like that?

Ivan looked to the floor. "My father taught me to defend myself."

"He did a very good job." The Captain set down his coffee.

The room was quiet except for the creaking of the bulkheads as the ship swayed with the waves.

"You understand I have to protect my ship and my men. Is there anything I should know about you, Ivan? Have you brought danger aboard my ship?"

Ivan leaned forward. "No, Captain. There is no danger to your ship . . . or your men."

The Captain stared at Ivan for a moment. "Good. You may go."

"Thank you, Captain." Ivan stood, put on his cap, and went through the door. He pulled the door closed behind him and heaved a deep sigh.

One of the cooks was walking by. "First time with the Captain?"

Ivan nodded.

"He's a good man. Takes good care of his ship and his

men." The cook walked off whistling.

Everyone knows.

Ivan found Joseph on the mess deck that evening.

"How did it go with the Captain?" asked Joseph over a bowl of stew.

"There aren't any secrets on this ship, are there?

Joseph laughed. "It may not seem like it to you now, but there are. You are new. Every new man is scrutinized, *mon ami*. Do not take it as an insult. In fact, if you do not enjoy it, it will get worse. Besides, this happens every time there is a scuffle."

"On and off the ship?"

"Yes, on the ship especially. Off the ship, if more than one crewmember is involved. The Captain allows no hostility. If there is a troublemaker, he is put off at the next port. There are no exceptions."

"Is he a tyrant?"

"No, *mon ami*, he is a fair man. A very fair man. He treats everyone the same. Feel honored. He did not tell you that you were leaving the ship, did he?"

"No."

Joseph reached out and rubbed Ivan's shoulder. "This is good. You have won his trust."

"How do you know?"

"Because, mon ami, he did not question me. If he had doubts, he would have."

Ivan nodded. "Is the stew good?"

"Good? Taste it for yourself. An opinion of food is relative."

"Is it one of the foods I should be eating?" Ivan asked suspiciously.

"Ah! You're worried about turning green?"

Ivan closed one eye and tilted his head.

"The sea is not rough enough. You are staggering a little, but you are not hopping on one foot."

"Does that happen before one turns green?"

"I know nothing, nothing at all," said Joseph with a smile.

Ivan went to the line, picking up a tray and bowl. He held the bowl out to the server who filled it half- way. "You can have as much as you want, but save room for dessert."

"What is it?" asked Ivan.

"Chocolate pudding. It is for you."

"For me?"

"Yes, in honor of your victory." The server winked.

"My victory?"

"At the cabaret. The Russian."

Ivan shook his head.

"You don't want it?" asked the server in surprise.

"No. I mean yes, but I don't understand."

"It's a tradition. Whenever a man wins a fight, he is honored."

"What if he loses?"

"He gets no dessert for the rest of the voyage, the server laughed at his joke."

Ivan walked away shaking his head.

"What was that?" asked Joseph.

When Ivan explained, Joseph laughed until his eyes were wet. "That's Eugene. He is having fun with you."

Ivan frowned. "You mean the dessert is not for me?"

"No, *mon ami*, it is for all of us. The menu has been planned for days."

Ivan looked at Eugene and shook his fist.

Eugene just laughed and returned the gesture.

"We work hard and we play hard," said Joseph. "I better get back on duty. Bring me some of your special chocolate pudding later." Joseph winked at Eugene and left the mess deck.

Back at the rail, Ivan watched the sea run past the ship. The water churning and darkening was hypnotic as the sun disappeared.

A familiar menacing voice broke his trance. "So, it's the fighter," sneered the Giant.

Ivan jumped. He turned to see the big man's eyes staring down at him. "I didn't hear you."

"You better be careful then. More than one man has been thrown overboard without a trace."

Ivan's eyes narrowed. *Is he threatening me?*

"Ah! You don't like what I said?" The man smirked. "Why don't you do something about it?"

Ivan ignored him and turned back toward the sea.

"Look at me when I talk to you," snarled the Giant, grabbing Ivan's shoulder and pulling him around.

Ivan strained to pull away. Pain shot through his shoulder as the Giant squeezed harder.

Grabbing Ivan's throat, he pushed Ivan into the bulkhead, and in a gruff voice the Giant whispered, "Vasile says hello, Stepan."

Ivan grimaced as the words penetrated his mind and an evil grin spread across the Giant's face. He let go of Ivan's throat and punched Ivan in the face. Blood flowed from Ivan's nose, over his lips, chin, and onto his shirt.

The Giant grunted out a laugh, threw Ivan to the deck, and walked away.

Ivan wiped his face with the back of his hand. He grabbed a rail and pulled himself unsteadily to his feet. Dragging himself to his compartment, he prayed no one would see him and that the space would be empty. He stopped the blood, cleansed his face, and changed his shirt. He wadded up the bloody shirt and stuffed it into his locker with the intention of disposing of it later. *Vasile says hello. Paris. My worst nightmare is coming true.*

Ivan went to the quartermaster's office. Joseph was bending over a map. Stepping in, Ivan said, "Are you busy?"

Joseph looked at Ivan with a curious glance. "What happened to your face?"

"It's nothing," replied Ivan, turning away. "I missed a step and fell down the ladder."

"Speak the truth."

"It's nothing. So, we're going to Paris," Ivan said, changing the subject. "How long will it take?"

"We will be there the morning after next. You will like Paris."

Ivan shook his head. "I'd better let you do your work or we may end up off course." *I wish we would go off course.*

"Sleep well, *mon ami.*"

"What about my nose? Everyone will see it."

"Maybe not. It may look better in the morning. If anyone says anything, tell them the truth—you fell down the ladder."

Ivan lay in his bunk, the swaying of the ship rocking him back and forth. The moonlight drifted gently through the portal. *I'm exhausted.* He closed his eyes and tried to push the parade of thoughts out of his mind. *Two days to Paris. How do I keep the Giant away from me? Where can I hide?* He wrestled with the thoughts until his body gave over to a restless sleep.

Chapter 33

Ivan skipped breakfast and went to the quartermaster's cabin again. *Help me God, Keep the Giant away from me.*

"Good morning, *mon ami*. Your nose looks as if nothing happened last night," said Joesph.

Ivan nodded.

"I missed you at breakfast," said Joseph.

"I wasn't hungry."

"Ah, the sea—she is playing with you. You'll get used to it."

"I hope so. Can you show me how you plot our course? I have nothing to do until this evening and it looks interesting," said Ivan.

"I suppose. I have finished what Captain needs unless he decides to change course. You think you might want to be a quartermaster?"

"Perhaps."

Ivan spent the rest of the day with Joseph.

"It's time to eat. Is your stomach better?" asked Ivan.

"I'm not hungry."

"Hungry or not, you need to eat, *mon ami*. That little bit of bread I brought you at noon is not enough to sustain you. You will be working hard tomorrow. The Captain is hiring some extra men to work in the hold in Paris. There will be little rest for the next two days." said Joseph.

"Why?"

"The Captain believes there is rough weather coming in and he wants to be at sea when it hits."

"How does he know?" quizzed Ivan.

"I don't know, but he is seldom wrong about the weather. Everyone, even me, will be working until the cargo is unloaded and new cargo is on board. There will not be any liberty until we are done, and then only one day. Instead of being there a week, we will only be there for three days. We must be at sea before the storm hits."

This is good. "I don't understand." Ivan scratched his head.

"If we are tied to the dock during a storm, the water can bash us against the pier or another ship and tear us to pieces. It is better to be at sea, fully loaded, where there is nothing to crash into."

The Captain called a meeting of the crew once they were tied up in port. "Gentlemen," said the Captain. "There will be no liberty until we have emptied our cargo and we are loaded for our voyage. We will be in port for only three days. Normally it would be seven, but we must be at sea before the storm shows her face. There will be no liberty until we are ready for the voyage. To make up for this inconvenience, I will pay an extra day's wage for your liberty here."

The men cheered.

"Now, get to work you landlubbers."

"I see what you mean about him being a good man," said Ivan.

"Ah, yes. This is why I have been onboard for four years and have no plans of going to another ship," replied Joseph. "There is an interesting bit of news."

"What is it?"

"The Giant is not on board."

Ivan shivered as a chill went down his spine. "Not on board? Was he washed overboard?"

"No, the Captain thinks he slipped over the side after we tied up. It was just before dawn when we came in."

I know where he went.

"I've never seen the men work this hard," said Joseph. "I know the extra day's pay has helped, but the Giant being gone is a bigger motivation, I think."

"I'm working harder myself and I'm not even going ashore," said Ivan.

"*Oui*! This cannot be. It is unheard of. You are beyond comprehension. All of Paris is at your feet. The women . . . the women, Ivan." Joseph put his hands to his forehead and shook his head. "I will never understand you, *mon ami*. We are going on a long voyage and you want stay aboard?"

Ivan laughed. "Where are we going?"

"To Boston . . . in America."

Ivan's heart jumped. He grabbed Joseph's shoulders. "America! Have you been to America?"

"Yes, twice." Joseph laughed.

"Tell me what it's like," demanded Ivan.

"I will have to tell you later," said Joseph. "We have to get this ship loaded. I do not understand you."

"So be it," smiled Ivan. "It isn't necessary for you to understand me."

"You are a crazy one, *mon ami*, crazy." Joseph walked off talking to himself and waving his hands in the air.

Several of the men were watching Joseph, and then looked at Ivan with questioning eyes.

Ivan shrugged.

The calm water reflected the bright sunlight and a slight breeze blew in from the south. Ivan leaned against the rail and imagined what Paris must be like. *It would be nice to be ashore with Joseph and the others. Paris is a large city, but still, they found me in Bayonne and even on the ship. Ferka said they never give up. I'm much safer here.*

Pushing the thoughts from his mind, Ivan enjoyed the view. The harbor, busy with ships being loaded and unloaded, fascinated him. Smaller craft carried small groups of people who had paid to tour the harbor. He noticed a boat coming toward the ship. *Tourists.* As it drew closer, an uneasy feeling churned in his stomach.

Those aren't sightseers. Squinting his eyes, he tried to make out the passengers. *They aren't sailors from the ship either.* He strained to see the occupants. His heart nearly stopped beating when he recognized the Giant sitting in the rear. Ivan slipped through a hatch and leaned against the bulkhead.

His heart beating fast and his breath short, he whispered "*Okhrana*."

"Permission to come aboard," asked one of the men.

"What is the nature of your business?" replied the officer on deck.

"We have an interest in Stepan Ivanov."

Ivan tried to become part of the ship.

"We have no one by that name," replied the officer.

"Grant us permission to come aboard, sir?"

"Permission denied!"

"May I speak to your captain? It's a matter of great urgency!"

Sweat dripped from Ivan's forehead. *Don't panic! No one knows me by that name! No one knows my past!*

"I'm the Captain. Why do you want to come aboard? You have been told there's no one with that name aboard this ship. What is your authority?"

"Perhaps there's a Nathan Hertzfield."

Ivan grabbed his chest trying to keep his heart from exploding. The sound of his real name drove his anxiety even higher.

"No, there's no one by that name aboard."

"Captain, I have seen this person with my own eyes," said the Giant. "He came on your ship at Bayonne. His name is Ivan. An *Okhrana* agent who fought him at the cabaret in Bayonne, identified him by his gold pocket watch. I spoke to this agent after the fight. I know he's onboard."

"Then I insist we be allowed to board so we can search

your ship," said the leader in the boat. "This is a dangerous man. He's a Russian Jew from Odessa who has interfered with the Russian Army and has committed an act of treason. He's a deserter. We're from the Russian *Okhrana*. Are you familiar with us?"

"Why should I be familiar with you? I'm not Russian," said the Captain.

"Perhaps if you were familiar with us, you would grant us permission to come aboard your ship, Captain," said the man with an air of authority.

"Are you threatening me, sir?" The Captain leaned forward.

"No, Captain. We wish only to arrest this man and take him back for trial. Don't deny us our right to find and capture him. We will force our way aboard if we have to."

"Are you associated in any way with Spain's Maritime department?"

"No. We're here by agreement between the Russian and French governments."

"Then you should know, sir, this vessel is registered with the country of Spain. If you step one foot onboard, you are committing an act of war with Spain and her allies."

"Captain, you're interfering with a treaty between the governments of Russia and France. You are in French waters. I don't think you have the authority to deny us permission to board!"

"Don't assume you know of my authority. This ship isn't the property of France or Russia. It isn't a military ship.

I'm the sole authority on this ship and I suggest you do not test me further." The Captain turned to his officer on deck saying, "Mr. Vega, alert the master at arms of this situation."

The officer blew a signal on his bosun whistle and almost immediately, there were a dozen armed men at the rail.

"Now sir, I suggest you return to where you came from without delay," said the Captain.

"Do you think this is wise, Captain?"

"Do you think it wise to delay your departure, sir?"

The man muttered a command over his shoulder and the boat turned and headed toward Paris.

Ivan's lungs pushed quick puffs of air through his parted lips. Wiping his brow with the back of a sweaty hand, he slumped. Feeling his body relax as the anxiety left him, he walked toward the ladder. He reached out a trembling hand and took the rail to steady himself. With care, he descended their steps slowly, went to his compartment, and lay down on his bunk.

Thank you God. Thank you.

Chapter 34

Ivan closed his eyes, but his thoughts wouldn't let him sleep. After what seemed like an eternity, the men came back from liberty. He focused on the sounds of their laughter and bragging of their exploits. Soon came the sounds of the ship being prepared to leave the dock. Then, it was quiet.

The ship rocked gently. The sound of water lapping against the ship relaxed him. He raised up on his elbow and looked out the portal. The ship was heading out to sea. He let out a deep sigh.

Just as he was dozing off, a sailor stepped through the hatch. "Ivan, the Captain would like to see you in his quarters."

What am I going to say to him?

Wiping the palms of his hands on his pants, Ivan looked at the door. The brass plate spelled "Captain" in black letters. Trembling, he knocked softly.

"Come in."

Ivan removed his hat and entered. "You want to see me, sir?"

"Yes, Ivan, I do. Be seated, please."

Ivan sat down. It was several moments before the Captain spoke.

What is he going to do with me?

"Ivan, we need to talk. I know most of the men on this ship as if they were my sons, but you're a stranger to me." He paused to light his pipe. After taking a puff, he placed his elbows on his knees and looked Ivan in the eyes. "There was an incident earlier today. I suspect you know the details, don't you?"

Ivan nodded.

The Captain proceeded as if he didn't see the nod. "Six men came to the ship in a boat and tried to board. I was summoned to the gangway. They were inquiring about a Russian Jew from Ukraine who deserted the Russian Army. They said they had reason to believe he was on my ship. They were part of the *Okhrana*. I would not let them come aboard."

He took a puff from his pipe, leaned back, and blew smoke into the air. His eyes followed the smoke for a moment and then he looked, again, into Ivan's eyes. "You told me you did not bring danger to my ship."

"I wasn't aware I had, Captain."

"They gave two names, Stepan Ivanov and Nathan Hertzfield. Yet, you come to me as Ivan Popov. Who are you, son?"

Ivan let out a heavy sigh. "Nathan Hertzfield."

"Why didn't you tell me the *Okhrana* knew you were on my ship?"

"The Giant attacked me one night after we left Bayonne. He threatened me and I was scared. I didn't know what to do." Ivan put his hands to his forehead and rubbed.

"Did Joseph know of this?"

"No, Captain, he knows nothing of my past. May I have a glass of water, sir?"

The Captain nodded at a pitcher and glass. "Help yourself, son. It's time for you to tell me the truth, Ivan. Why were they looking for you?"

Ivan hesitated.

"I'm waiting, Ivan."

"I am the man they wanted, Captain but what they told you isn't true. I mean not all of it. It's true I am a defector from the Russian Army, but I'm not a criminal." Ivan straightened up in his chair.

"You're not a criminal?"

"No, sir. I am most assuredly not a criminal."

"This is like a puzzle, son. I think you had better start at the beginning."

"It's a long story, Captain. It started five years ago."

"Well, Ivan. We have sixteen days before we dock in Boston. Do you think this is enough time to tell me."

"Yes, sir."

"Let me get some more water and coffee." The Captain summoned the steward and made the arrangements. While waiting for the steward, he filled his pipe with a fresh stock of tobacco.

Ivan wiped his brow. *God, help me through this.*

The steward filled the Captain's cup and served the two men some pie, then he quietly slipped out of the cabin.

The Captain lit his pipe and leaned back in his chair. "I'm

ready, young man."

Ivan glanced at the clock on the cabin wall—1922.

When he finished hours later, the Captain stood, walked to the hatch, and opened it. Leaning against the bulkhead, he stared at the sea for several minutes.

Sweat ran down Ivan's face and dripped onto his shirt. *What is he going to do?*

The Captain returned to his chair, leaned back, and tapped the stem of his pipe against his teeth. He leaned forward and placed his elbows on his knees. Again he looked Ivan directly in his eyes. "I'm sorry for what has happened to you, Ivan. I understand why you want to go to America. I understand your secrecy. It isn't the first time I've had to take a stand for one of my men and I'm sure it won't be the last. These are troubled times for Jews. I'm afraid there are dark clouds on the horizon. America may be the answer for you. I don't know. Only you can decide this. I'll continue to help you get there. Is there anything else I should know? Is there anything else that can bring potential trouble to my ship and crew?"

"No, Captain. I've told you everything. I give you my word."

"Will you be able to work with my Russian sailors? Notwithstanding, the incident with the Giant—he was only on the ship a month—the others have been with me for several years. I do know them."

"Yes, sir. You've told me you know your men. I believe if they were any danger to me you would know. I believed the Giant was a happenstance at first, but after the incident in

Bayonne, he was on to me."

"I thank God for keeping you safe."

"Yes, sir. Thank God."

"You don't need to worry, Ivan. This ship is a sanctuary for you, but you must know there will be questions about today's incident. Word travels quickly. This is the second incident that has involved you. The men will be curious. How you handle their questions is up to you. They respect you."

"I know, Captain. I'll be straightforward with them."

"That's all I need to know, Ivan. We won't speak of this incident again unless you wish to talk to me."

"Thank you, sir."

"And when you get to America . . . ."

Ivan waited.

"You can change your name to Nathan or any other name you wish," the Captain said with a wide grin.

Ivan nodded.

"There is one other thing I'd like to speak to you about."

"Yes, sir." Ivan looked at him quizzically.

"You have been through a lot for such a young man—the loss of your father at a young age, kidnapping, being separated from your mother and brother, betrayed by someone you trusted, forced to abscond, and risk your life. I have a friend who was also betrayed by someone close to him. This friend was the son of a king. The betrayal cost him his life."

"I'm sorry, sir. Who was he?

"His name *is* Jesus."

His name is Jesus? How can that be if he was killed?

"I see that what I said puzzles you, Ivan. We have several days ahead of us. We'll talk more."

Ivan nodded and left the cabin. Closing the hatch behind him, he went to the rail and watched the sea churn as the ship steamed through the water. *Is it really over? Is the Okhrana really behind me? Am I truly free?* Suddenly everything looked clearer—the sky, the sea. He listened to the sound of the sea and the ship steaming through the water. The air smelled cleaner. He smiled to himself. *Thank you, God. Thank you so very much.*